THE SWEETEST FEELING

Poppy manages the traditional and very popular tearoom in Bramleys Garden Centre, which is owned by Jim Mabey. When Jim's eldest son, Andrew, returns from London with a new girlfriend and new ideas in tow, Poppy's business and her contented lifestyle are threatened. To complicate matters even more, she and Andrew were once in love — and Poppy soon realises that her feelings are unchanged. Can Andrew be persuaded that his future happiness lies with Poppy and Bramleys?

1

Poppy's tongue flicked between her teeth as she concentrated on the cake and the icing bag. L-E-M-O, she reached the last letter when an excited squawk from behind made her jump and the N trailed across the cake.

'Ella!' Poppy spun round. 'Look what you've made me do!'

'Oh, I'm sorry.' Ella's face was flushed but her blue eyes sparkled. 'Really, Poppy, I didn't see what you were doing.'

Poppy sighed, carefully lifted the messy icing from the cake and made another attempt on the N.

'There.' She put down the icing bag and wiped her hands roughly on a cloth. 'Finished. It doesn't show too much.' She examined the result. 'Lucky I managed to get the cherry one done before you started yelping.' She lifted

1

the cake carefully and placed it on a glass cake stand. 'Now, what's happened?'

Her friend kept glancing towards the doorway into the tearoom. 'Nothing's happened. I've just seen the most gorgeous man!'

'You've only been married for six months,' said Poppy in mock outrage. 'You shouldn't be looking at gorgeous men. What's wrong with Chris? Are you tired of him already?'

'I may be a married woman, but I can still look.'

'All right. As long as you just look. Where is this Adonis?'

'He's probably gone now,' said Ella, with another glance towards the door. 'He was in the tearoom with Jim.'

Poppy glanced at her sharply. 'With Jim? What did he look like?'

'Tall, broad-shouldered, dreamy eyes . . . oh!' She broke off as Jim Mabey, the owner of Bramleys Garden Centre appeared in the doorway, with the Adonis behind him.

2

'Andy!' Poppy stared in amazement. Jim stepped aside and Poppy rushed across the room and flung her arms around the young man's neck.

'Hello, Poppy.' Andrew flushed, gently disengaging her clinging arms and drew forwards the elegant young woman waiting behind him.

'This is Selena. Selena, Poppy, an old schoolfriend of mine.'

Schoolfriend! Poppy stared at him. Surely they'd been a bit more than that.

Selena, a vision in a red dress which clung to every graceful curve, and an expensive black and white jacket, held out her hand. Poppy, conscious of her flushed face and the sticky icing sugar between her fingers, rubbed her hands on her apron before taking the other girl's cool fingers.

'What a lovely smell of cakes,' said Selena. 'Do you make them?'

'Poppy makes wonderful cakes,' Jim broke in with enthusiasm.

'I wouldn't know where to start,' said Selena, making it sound like a virtue.

'What are you doing back here?' asked Poppy. 'I thought you were settled in London.'

'I've come back to see Dad.' The young man put an affectionate arm round his father's shoulders. 'And to look round the old place. See if there's been any changes.'

'Mind if we look round, Poppy?' asked his father.

'Of course not. It is your tearoom after all.'

'Only for a while longer,' he smiled. 'As soon as you have enough money, we'll do a deal.'

Selena was looking enquiringly from one to the other.

'The tearoom is part of the garden centre,' explained Jim. 'But Poppy wants to own it herself instead of just managing it. We've agreed a price. As soon as she has enough, it's hers. And judging by the success of the place, that won't be long.'

'I see,' said Selena, thoughtfully, looking around and taking in the

4

wrought iron tables, flanked by comfortable chairs, the wallpaper with its design of poppies in cornfields, the soft orangey red drapes and the pretty mob cap lamp shades.

'Looks a bit different from the old place,' said Andrew. 'That was dingy brown paint and dull wooden chairs and tables. You must have spent quite a bit on it, Dad.'

'It's been worth it,' said Jim Mabey. 'It's becoming a little goldmine, and all due to Poppy here.'

Poppy smiled at him warmly. 'Go and sit down and Ella will bring you some tea.'

Her friend was hovering behind her, waiting to be introduced. 'Would you like some cake with your tea?' she asked.

The men agreed enthusiastically but Selena gave a faint shudder. 'I never eat carbs.'

Ella followed Poppy into the kitchen while the others chose a table.

'Is he an old flame of yours?' she asked.

'Not exactly.' Poppy put cups and saucers on to a tray and filled a teapot. 'We were at school together. After school, we used to help Jim in the garden centre. He was building it up then and glad of the help. We were glad of the pocket money.'

Ella gave her an old-fashioned look, but asked, 'Why didn't he come into the business?' She cut two generous slices of lemon cake.

'I don't know.' Poppy added a jug of milk and a bowl of sugar to the tray. 'He certainly had green fingers. But suddenly he became interested in computers. He went away to university and then straight into a job in London.'

'It's funny, I never knew Jim had an older son.'

'He doesn't talk about him a great deal. And of course, he has his other family.' Poppy picked up the tray and handed it to Ella. 'Jim's proud of him, of course, but I'm sure he'd hoped Andy would join him in the business. He doesn't understand why anyone would prefer to live in London.'

Ella took the tray into the tearoom and was soon back.

'He's a dish,' she said, 'but I don't like the look of that Selena. Why hasn't Andy been home for visits?'

'He has,' said Poppy, 'but they really were flying ones. We didn't see him. And he worked in Paris for a year. He's a real whizzkid, I can tell you. Much too grand for the likes of us.'

She turned away and began to tip vegetables into a steamer. She felt really annoyed with Andy. The first time they'd met in three years and he treated her like that — almost pushing her away. She supposed he was influenced by the presence of the glamorous Selena.

Poppy looked through the serving hatch into the tearoom. Jim, Andy and Selena were talking with animation. Andy had a notepad in front of him and was writing as they talked. Poppy went over and offered more tea. Only Jim accepted.

'I was just reminding Drew that we have to call and see his friends at Oak Farm,' said Selena, gathering up her bag and gloves. 'Goodbye, Poppy. It was lovely to meet you. I'm sure we shall see lots of each other. Come along, Drew.'

Andy gave Poppy's arm a slight squeeze as he passed and he and Selena left the tearoom. Poppy and Jim watched them go.

'Drew!' exclaimed Poppy, in a tone of outrage. She caught Jim's eye and they both began to laugh.

'Wait here,' she said, 'I'll get us both some tea.'

'Is there something I should know?' she asked, as she settled herself at the table with her tea.

Jim passed a hand over his face and gave her a rueful smile. 'You know I went to the hospital for a check-up two weeks ago?'

'You said everything was all right.'

'I lied.'

Poppy's head jerked up. 'Everything is not all right? Why didn't you tell me?'

Jim looked down at the table. 'I need an operation. I'm a coward. I couldn't tell anyone because I thought if I didn't talk about it, it would go away.'

Poppy put a hand over his brown, weather beaten one and gave it a squeeze. 'You're not a coward. That's a natural reaction.'

'They want me to go into hospital soon. I sent for Andrew. He'd said that he was between contracts so I wondered whether he would take charge here until I'm better.'

'Isn't he a bit out of things? He hasn't worked here for years. Annie must know more about it than Andy.'

'Annie has enough to do with the children.' Jim's voice softened. 'Fifteen-year-old twins are a full time job. She's quite happy for Andy to be in charge.'

Poppy thought of Jim's second wife, fair, plump and placid. She wouldn't want her comfortable life disrupted by the task of running the garden centre. Poppy liked Annie, but she had to admit to herself that she thought the

9

other woman just a little lazy.

'I don't suppose Andrew will be 'hands on', more a supervisor. I have Chris to do the day-to-day planning, and I know the rest of the staff will rally round.'

They both sat silent, thinking. Then Poppy said quietly, 'And Selena?'

'Selena was a surprise.' Jim grimaced. 'Andrew said she's a brilliant accountant and will be useful in the office.'

'You mean, Drew says,' said Poppy, and they both began to laugh again.

'It's what he's called in London,' Jim said between laughs. 'I shall never call him that.'

'And to me, he'll always be Andy,' said Poppy.

Jim wiped his eyes. 'You've done me good, lass,' he said. 'I needed a laugh.'

'Well I'm sure they'll leave me alone,' said Poppy. 'They won't have any interest in a teashop. Selena can't make cakes and doesn't eat carbs.'

Laughing again, they separated, Jim to return to his plants and Poppy to supervise lunch. Customers were beginning to come in and she had spent half an hour with Jim. She hurried into the kitchen.

Ella was carving a joint. She glanced up as Poppy came in.

'Sorry,' said Poppy. 'Jim had something to tell me. We'll talk about it when the rush is over. Are we nearly ready? Tell me what needs doing.'

'I'm a miracle worker,' laughed Ella. 'Everything's done.'

Poppy glanced through the serving-hatch as she changed into a gleaming white apron.

'Jim's mum has just come in with Mr Bevington Wood.'

'Of course.' Ella gave a little giggle. 'Do you think there's a romance there?'

'I hope so. They're a lovely couple. We could have the wedding here.'

A few days later, Jim went reluctantly into hospital. Poppy held a little party for him the evening before. He'd danced with everyone, determined to put the coming ordeal out of his mind.

'I hope he'll be all right,' said Poppy to Ella, as they uncovered plates of sandwiches, quiches and pieces of chicken. 'He's so nervous. You don't expect such a big man to have nerves.'

'You're very fond of him, aren't you?' said Ella.

'I've known him a long time. He's always been very supportive. He must be all right.' Her voice broke on the last word.

Ella gave her a hug as Chris came into the kitchen. 'Anything wrong?' he asked.

'Poppy's worried about Jim,' said his wife.

'He'll be fine,' said Chris. 'He's strong as an ox. Don't show him you're upset. He's having a good time.'

As he spoke, Jim appeared in the kitchen doorway. He was slightly the worse for drink.

'Where's my Poppy? I want to dance with my little Poppy.'

'All right.' Poppy forced a laugh. 'But no more drinks. What will the hospital say if we have to carry you in only half sober? One dance, then you'll have several coffees with your supper.'

He put his arm round her waist and swept her into the dancing.

Andy and Selena arrived late. Selena was poured into a navy grosgrain dress that screamed 'designer'.

Poppy smoothed down the fitted green skirt of her own dress and wished she was a little taller and a great deal more willowy.

She watched them out of the corner of her eye while pretending to supervise the cutting of Jim's *Good Luck* cake. Selena was holding Andy's arm as if she had no intention of relinquishing him to any old schoolfriend.

Then Poppy noticed Ella whispering to Chris and giving him a little push in the direction of Selena. To Poppy's amazement, they began to dance.

Ella crossed behind Poppy on her way to the kitchen. 'See how I have your interests at heart,' she murmured. 'I've sacrificed my beloved for you. I've separated Selena from Andy.'

'Why . . . ?' Poppy turned to answer her and found herself looking at Andy.

'Will you dance with me, Poppy?'

Surprised, but without speaking, she went into his arms and they began to circle the room.

'You've grown up,' he said.

'So have you.'

'But you look so different tonight.'

'Different from what? Different from my sticky appearance in the kitchen or different from when I was muddy in the garden centre? I'm dressed up tonight, or hadn't you noticed?'

'Oh, I noticed all right.' Andy gave the deep laugh she remembered so well. His arm tightened round her waist. 'It's lovely to see you again, Poppy.'

She wanted to say, 'You could have seen me on any of your infrequent visits home.' She wanted to remind him that it was four years since they'd met. Four years! She hadn't forgotten him. He'd been her first love and despite other boyfriends since then, the only one who meant anything.

'You've changed your hair colour,' he said.

'Everyone does.' Her tone was defensive.

'I'm not criticising,' he said, hastily. 'It's lovely. It glows like rich marmalade.' He picked up a strand and twisted it round his finger. As he did so, Selena and Chris danced past them. The look Selena gave Poppy could have sliced through her like a knife.

Andy smiled down at Poppy. 'Oops! That will take some explaining.'

'Perhaps you'd better go and make your peace,' she said. 'I think I'm needed in the kitchen. Excuse me.' The party broke up soon after that.

Poppy arrived at Bramleys early the next morning to wave Jim off. He'd insisted on paying a final visit to check on staff arrangements and take a final look around.

A subdued Jim kissed Poppy and climbed into Andrew's car. She waved until the car was out of sight then went slowly into her tearoom. She'd have a

15

cup of tea then look at the day's menus. If she made an early start on preparations, she and Ella would have an easier day.

When Andrew returned, he came into the tearoom to look for Poppy. 'He's settled in,' he reported. 'Now we just wait.' They looked at each other. 'He'll be fine,' said Andrew. 'We must make sure everything carries on just as if he was here. I don't want to interfere with your business, but if you need anything, you know where to find me.'

Poppy smiled at him. 'Thank you, Andy. I'm glad you've come back.'

'It's only for a while,' he reminded her. 'As soon as Dad is better and stronger, I shall go back to London. I've kept my flat on, I don't want to burn any boats.'

'And Selena?' she inquired, diffidently.

Andrew flushed. 'Selena is her own woman. She does as she likes. Perhaps she'll stay, perhaps she won't.' He stood up and gave her a little wave. 'I must go and report to Annie. See you later.'

When he'd left, Poppy sat and thought. What did his remarks mean? Was Selena his girlfriend or wasn't she? And did it matter? Andy had shown no interest in her.

Ella's arrival put an end to her speculations and they went into the kitchen to start the day.

★   ★   ★

Life was quiet for a while until one afternoon, Selena appeared in the tearoom. There was a lull between lunch and afternoon tea. Selena strolled around looking at the drapes and décor, studying the pictures and flowers. She ended up in front of the board displaying lunchtime *Specials*.

Poppy watched her surreptitiously through the serving-hatch, then she emerged from the kitchen.

'Good afternoon, Selena. Have you come for afternoon tea?'

17

'Just a cup of tea, please. No food.'

'Of course, the carbs,' murmured Poppy.

Selena looked at her sharply but Poppy managed to keep her face straight.

'Bring an extra cup,' called Selena, as Poppy went into the kitchen. 'We haven't had a chat since I arrived.'

Poppy made a face at Ella, but obeyed and carried the tray to Selena's table. She sat opposite the other girl.

'How are you enjoying your break in the country,' she asked, pleasantly. 'You must find it very different from London.'

'I don't enjoy it.' Selena picked up the teapot. 'You'll be surprised to know that I was brought up in the country — in a little village. I escaped when I was seventeen. I never want to go back.'

'Really.' Poppy studied her. No, pale cream clothes and long red nails were not country wear. 'So what made you come here?'

Selena shot a look at her. 'Andrew, of course. We've been together for two years. I didn't want to desert him.'

Or give him the chance to desert you, thought Poppy.

'You and Drew were — friends once? Close friends?' Selena was watching her intently.

'Does it matter?' asked Poppy.

'It does to me.'

'Why don't you ask Andy?' She used the name deliberately.

'I'm asking you.'

Poppy thought for a while before answering. She could pretend there'd been more between them then there was and annoy Selena. But if questioned, Andy would deny it and after the incident with her hair during the dance, Selena probably had a right to be touchy. After all, she looked upon Andy as her property.

'Just school friends,' she said. 'We went around together, but mostly with a group of friends.'

Selena seemed satisfied.

They sipped their tea. Poppy wondered what they were to chat about.

Selena looked around the room. 'This — décor — is your choice?'

Poppy took a deep breath to steady her voice. 'Yes. You disapprove?'

Selena gave a short laugh. 'It's not for me to disapprove, though as a matter of fact, country style is not my preference.'

Poppy looked around the tearoom. She had spent hours tramping around shops, carefully matching the orangey red drapes to the poppy pattern on the wallpaper. She'd persuaded Jim to change the window glass for small diamond panes. Together they'd decided on wrought iron tables with soft red cushions on the chairs. She was immensely satisfied with the result and so, to judge by the number of people who visited regularly, were her customers. She looked at Selena.

'So what would you change?'

Selena looked at her. 'You really want to know?'

Poppy nodded.

Selena took a deep breath. 'Everything.'

Poppy looked at her in horror but said nothing.

'I'd have beige linen curtains,' said Selena, 'and plain cream walls, with perhaps some chocolate coloured beams. Wooden tables with glass tops, wooden chairs and do away with those cushions. The flowers and pictures would have to go, of course, and the carpet on the floor. Tiles would look better.' She looked at Poppy. 'Something like that. Can you imagine it?'

'Oh yes.' Poppy's voice was tight. 'I can imagine it.'

'And the menu,' Selena gestured towards the blackboard. 'I don't think toasted sandwiches or teacakes are very imaginative. We could try paninis and baguettes.'

'My customers like toasted sandwiches,' said Poppy, defiantly.

'Yes, I've seen your customers.' Selena's expression was scathing. 'Old biddies from the retirement home and peasants from round about. With new décor and an up-to-date menu, you could attract a completely different class of customer.'

'But I'm happy with my customers. They're loyal. And they're satisfied with the place as it is. I'm sorry you don't like it, but I do and so do my customers. I won't change a thing.'

'We'll see about that,' said Selena, sweetly. 'While Jim is away, I'm in charge of finances. With some changes here, we could make far more money. I'm sure Jim would be pleased if he saw an improvement in profits when he came back.'

'Jim agrees with everything I've done. He helped me choose a lot of the furnishings. I don't think he gave you the right to make changes.'

'Drew will approve my ideas,' said Selena, confidently. 'Don't let's fight about it. I just want you to consider some changes.'

Poppy poured out some more tea, quelling the urge to throw it at the

other girl. Of all the arrogant, self-satis-
fied . . .

'Just one more thing that occurred to me,' said Selena, 'weddings. Wedding receptions.'

'We do wedding receptions. Several each year. Not grand ones, of course, but for smaller weddings, the brides like this room.'

'Mmm. I thought of a marquee. There's plenty of room in the field behind Jim's house. With a marquee, we could do larger receptions.'

Poppy was silent.

'Next time you have a bride in, suggest it.' Selena finished her tea. 'Do a little poll. I think you'll be surprised.' She stood up. 'I've enjoyed our chat, Poppy. Promise me you'll think about my suggestions. 'Bye.' She fluttered her fingers and left the café.

Ella popped out of the kitchen. 'Can I see steam coming out of your ears?'

'I need to cool down before I tell you what she said.' Poppy stared miserably

23

ahead. 'I wonder whether she has the authority to make any changes here.'

'Here's Andrew coming.' Ella glanced towards the door. 'Ask him.'

Andrew came straight over to Poppy's table and sat down opposite her. He was smiling nervously. 'Selena tells me you two have had a chat. What did you think of her ideas. She's go-ahead. I expect you'll need time to think about them.'

Poppy looked at him for a few minutes without speaking, then she said, 'Andy, has Jim given Selena authority to make changes here?'

'Not exactly.' The words came out reluctantly. 'But I'm sure he'll approve any ideas which increase profits.'

'I don't need to think about her ideas,' said Poppy. 'I don't approve of any of them. My tearoom is successful. Jim is happy about it and so am I. I'm sorry, Andy, but you can tell her that from me.'

Andrew looked across the table, his brows drawn together in a scowl.

'Selena only wants to help. This place is behind the times, out of date, not modern. Together we can change it for the better.' He stood up. 'And while we're about it, Poppy, would you please not call me Andy! I don't mind Andrew, but I'm known as Drew now.' He gave her a thin smile and left the room.

2

One morning, Ella arrived for work without her usual sunny smile. Poppy watched her covertly for a while as she moved about the kitchen making preparations for the days' meals. At last, she had to speak. There was obviously something wrong.

'Do you feel all right, Ella?'

'Yes. Why?' The reply was unusually brusque.

'You seem quiet.'

'Can't I be quiet for a change?'

There was a silence between them for a while, then with a loud sniff, Ella sank on to a chair and put her face in her hands.

'Ella.' Poppy was beside her in a second. 'Ella. Something is wrong. Tell me.'

'It's Chris.' The voice came from behind her hands. 'We've had a row.

26

The first one since . . . '

Poppy put an arm round her friend. 'All married couples have rows. Was it a bad one?'

'Bad enough. In a way, it was about you. I said he was disloyal and . . . oh a lot of other things.'

'About me?' Poppy pulled up a chair and sat opposite her friend.

Ella wiped her eyes. 'Chris and I went out for a pub meal with Selena and Andrew last night.'

Poppy looked at her with widened eyes. 'I didn't know you were on those terms.'

'Nothing to do with me,' said Ella, hastily. 'Andrew and Chris fixed it up. I didn't know until he got home last night and told me to get ready to go out. We had a nice meal but Chris was a pain, laughing at Andrew's feeble jokes and agreeing with everything he said. When we got home, he started again about how clever Andrew was, how well organised, what brilliant ideas he had.'

'I got annoyed because I don't think

Andrew, or Selena, have been very nice to you, and I said so. One thing led to another and he didn't even kiss me goodnight.'

She looked so tragic that Poppy had difficulty in keeping a solemn expression on her face. It was obviously very important to Ella. She stood up.

'I'll make us some tea. Dry your eyes. I'll bet Chris is as unhappy as you about it. He'll be in soon to see you, I'm sure.' She filled the kettle. 'Guess where I went last evening? You won't guess, so I'll tell you. St George's Court!'

'St George's Court? The retirement flats? Why ever did you go there?' Ella dabbed at her eyes.

'It was Mr Bevington Wood's birthday. They were having a party for him. I met him on my way home and he invited me.'

'Did you enjoy yourself?' Ella was smiling now.

'I did. I really did. Of course, so many of the people at the party are our customers, I knew them already. We had a lovely buffet and then we danced.'

'Danced!' Ella was highly amused.

'Certainly. I danced twice with Mr Bevington Wood. He's a wonderful dancer. Don't forget he was on the stage in his youth.'

As she lifted the cup to her lips, she glanced out of the window. From there, she could see across to the field behind Jim's house.

'Ella, what's that man doing?'

'Man? Where?' Ella stood up and went to the window. 'He's measuring the field, isn't he? Why would . . . ?'

'Measuring the field? Oh, no!' Poppy remembered her conversation with Selena. 'If it's what I think it is . . . ' Poppy removed her apron and marched out of the room. From the window, Ella saw her cross the field and speak to the man.

'What exactly are you doing?' Poppy's voice was cold; she knew the answer.

'Measuring.' The man straightened

up and wrote something on his clipboard. 'Measuring for your marquee. That is, I'm measuring to see that you have enough room when you come to hire one of our marquees.'

'And who asked you to do this?'

He consulted his board again. 'Miss Selena Pembury. Isn't that you?'

'It certainly is not. But I shall go and see her now.'

Poppy marched across the field to the office of the garden centre. Selena was inside, working on the computer. She looked cool and efficient. She looked up as Poppy came in. The slight smile of welcome disappeared completely as she saw Poppy's expression.

'There's a man measuring the field for a marquee,' said Poppy.

'Oh, he's come, has he. Good,' said Selena.

'I told you I don't want a marquee for weddings,' Poppy began. 'Weddings are nothing to do with the garden centre. Why must you interfere?'

She was aware that Selena was

looking towards the door. Poppy turned. Andrew stood there.

'What on earth is going on? I could hear you from the pottery. Good thing we have very few customers in yet.'

'I really don't know why I bother.' Selena got in the first word before Poppy could draw breath. 'I'm only trying to help to increase her profits. She takes all my suggestions the wrong way.'

'I don't need her help or her suggestions,' said Poppy between clenched teeth. 'Tell her to let me run my business in my own way.'

'It's not exactly your business,' said Selena smoothly, 'not yet anyway. At the moment it still belongs to Bramley Garden Centre.'

Andrew came into the room and looked from one to the other.

'My father would be most distressed if he knew that this was happening,' he said. 'For his sake, would you please try to get on together. It won't be for long. Poppy, forget the marquee idea. Carry

31

on in your own way.'

Poppy was too keyed up by her argument with Selena, to speak. She looked from one to the other, turned on her heel and marched out of the office.

'Well, thank you for your support,' she heard Selena say, as she walked out. Poppy passed the man with the clipboard without a word and carried on to her tearoom.

Ella looked up from beating eggs as Poppy entered the kitchen.

'You don't look very happy,' said Ella.

'I've just had a row with Selena.' She told Ella what had happened in the office.

'He stuck up for you,' Ella commented.

'She won't forgive me for that. I heard her start on Andy as I left. Oh, let's forget about them both. We have work to do. Where's Annoushka?'

Annoushka was their Polish waitress, hard-working and a favourite with the customers, but an erratic timekeeper.

Ella looked through the window.

'Here she is. Rushing as usual.'

The girl gave them each a beaming smile, hastily tied on her apron, grabbed a pad and pencil from the table and disappeared into the café.

Poppy decided to visit Jim in hospital that evening. She would go straight from work so that she wouldn't bump into Selena and Andrew if they also chose to go that evening.'

It was strange to see Jim lying in a hospital bed, his weather-beaten face so brown against the whiteness of the sheets and pillows.

'You look remarkably healthy,' she joked. 'Are you sure you should be here?'

'He'll need a good rest,' said the nurse who overheard her words, 'Don't encourage him to think he can leave.'

'How're things?' asked Jim.

'Fine,' said Poppy. 'We've barely noticed you're not there.'

'What about Selena? She's not interfering, is she?'

'She's doing her job, I'm doing mine.'

'I'm glad you're getting on. I've been worried about you. She's an interfering little madam and likes her own way.'

'Don't worry about a thing,' Poppy reassured him. 'Concentrate on getting well. I've brought you some grapes.' Poppy reached into her bag. 'You're supposed to bring grapes to invalids, aren't you?'

'Very kind, but I'd rather a box of cigars,' he growled.

She thought it best not to stay too long, so after a short chat, she left, promising to come again soon.

She passed the coffee bar on her way out, and on an impulse, decided to have a cup before returning home. She found a table and sat down, glad of the rest.

'Are you on your way in or out?' came a voice behind her. She spun round.

'Out,' she said, shortly.

'May I join you?' Andrew took a seat

opposite. 'How was he?'

'Quiet. Sleepy.'

Andrew looked at her as if unsure how to ask something.

'Don't worry, I didn't mention this morning,' she said. 'I told him everything was fine.'

'Thank you for not mentioning it.' He drank his coffee. 'I don't think bringing Selena from London with me was such a good idea.'

Poppy looked at him in silence.

'She misses the city,' he went on. 'She's not a country girl at heart.'

Poppy drank her coffee and looked at him over the rim of her cup.

'I don't know what to do,' he said, wretchedly. 'We row all the time. She wants me to go back to London, but how can I?'

'Chris could take charge. He's more than capable.'

'Of course he is, but Dad wanted me to look after the place. And besides,' he looked down at the floor, 'I'm beginning to enjoy it. I'd forgotten how much I used to love messing about with plants and soil.' He looked up at Poppy. 'We both enjoyed it, didn't we?'

'That was several years ago. You're a different person now.'

'But am I? I don't know. Selena complains that I seem more and more satisfied to live in a village and run the garden centre. She thinks I should be more ambitious.'

He seemed to want to confide in her, but Poppy hardened her heart. Selena was his girlfriend; he must deal with her. She stood up.

'I must go.' She wasn't going to use his name. 'Mrs Beaton will be waiting for her meal. She's been alone all day.'

'Mrs Beaton?'

'My cat. I'll see you in the morning. Goodnight.' Feeling rather unkind, but still very hurt, Poppy left the hospital.

★　★　★

'Have you seen Selena lately?' Poppy asked Ella a week later. 'She must be

36

keeping a low profile. It's not like her. But I haven't seen her for days.'

Ella stared at her. 'I thought you knew. She's gone back to London. Didn't Andrew tell you?'

'I haven't spoken to him for days.' Poppy stood gazing out of the window. 'Gone back to London. Do you mean for good?'

'No such luck. Just a visit, I think.'

Poppy began to hum a little tune as she finished laying the tables. Possibly the delights of London would keep Selena there, perhaps for good. She closed her eyes tightly. Please let it happen, she prayed.

She was loading dishes into the dishwasher when she became aware of raised voices in the tearoom. She looked towards Ella. 'What on earth . . . ?'

Annoushka ran in, her lips trembling. 'They are horrible, those boys. They make fun of me when I tell them . . . is not permitted.'

'What boys?' Poppy straightened up and went to the serving hatch.

'They are over there.'

Three large, rather stupid looking youths lounged at the table on the far side of the room. They were laughing raucously and two of them were smoking.

Luckily, only two more tables were occupied but the people sitting there were obviously embarrassed and trying hard to pretend they hadn't noticed anything.

'Ella, get Chris and Brian,' Poppy said over her shoulder and with a determined expression on her face, marched into the tearoom.

'I believe you have been told we don't allow smoking in here,' she began.

They ignored her and continued to laugh at each other in a gormless way.

Poppy repeated her remark and added, 'If you've finished your meal, perhaps you would like to leave.'

The leader of the three turned towards her and slowly got to his feet. He was over six feet tall, thin and angular. He towered over Poppy. 'You talking to us?' he asked.

Poppy stood her ground. 'Yes. I'd like you to leave now, if you don't mind.'

'Well I do mind. I want another cup of coffee. You sell coffee, so go and get me one.' He turned and smirked at his companions.

'I don't want to serve you anything else, I want you to go,' said Poppy.

'And who's going to make us?'

The door opened and Chris came in. Behind him was Brian, a large and burly gardener whose looks belied his gentle nature. The two men came over to Poppy and stood, one either side of her.

'Any problems?' asked Chris.

'I hope not. These — gentlemen — are leaving.'

The three got to their feet. 'We'll be back,' said the leader with an attempt at bravado.'

'I shouldn't bother,' said Chris. 'This isn't really your sort of place, is it?'

'Thank you,' said Poppy, when the

three youths had shuffled out.

Poppy apologised to the other patrons then led the way to the kitchen. 'Can we get you anything?'

'Not for me, but I'm sure Brian would like some cake.' Chris patted the large gardener on the shoulder. Brian gave an answering grin and Poppy reached for the chocolate cake.

★ ★ ★

She was locking up that evening when Andrew appeared. 'Busy today?' he asked.

'Very.' She checked the fridges and switched off the kitchen light.

'I suppose you heard that Selena has gone back to London for a few days.' He was trying to sound offhand as if it wasn't really important.

'Just a few days?'

'I don't know how long she'll be away. Probably only a few days.' He took the key from Poppy, locked the tearoom and gave her the key again, falling into step beside her as she walked to her car.

'Um, Poppy, would you have dinner with me one night, say tomorrow?'

She looked up at him. Was this a case of when the cat's away, the mice will play?

He was gazing at her anxiously. 'I'd really like it. There's some good restaurants in Flaxton.'

She relented. 'Very well. But not in Flaxton. We'll have it at my house. I'll cook you a real English roast. None of that foreign stuff you live on in London.'

'But I wanted to take you out. Give you a rest from cooking.'

'I love cooking. My house or nothing.'

He smiled widely and opened her car door. 'It's a date. What time?'

Poppy drove home planning the meal. She'd have to slip out tomorrow morning to shop. She'd made some carrot and coriander soup yesterday for the tearoom. Some of that would make a good starter. Then beef and roast potatoes. Cheese and biscuits to follow, or would he like something sweet? Sherry trifle, perhaps.

Before she knew it she was home, and Mrs Beaton was rushing down the path to meet her and wrap herself round Poppy's ankles.

★   ★   ★

Andrew's large frame seemed to fill the little sitting-room of Poppy's cottage. She went into the kitchen to check on the meal and when she returned, he was prowling round the room picking up a photograph here, an ornament there, or sliding a book from the bookcase and flicking through the pages.

He started guiltily as she came into the room. 'Your life,' he said, 'in one room. I'm sorry to be nosy, I was just interested.' He pointed to a framed school photograph. 'That's you in the front row and me just behind.'

She smiled and joined him in front of the photograph. 'There's Mr Gunter. Remember him? He was always sucking throat sweets.'

'And Miss Pennington. She was so stern.'

Poppy handed him a bottle of wine, a corkscrew and two glasses. 'Dinner won't be long. Sit down.'

He made himself comfortable in a soft, squashy armchair. Immediately, Mrs Beaton jumped on to his lap.

'That's her chair,' said Poppy. 'She thinks you are a cushion.' She tried in vain to remove the big cat. 'Your clothes!' she said. 'She's been brushed but her hairs get everywhere.'

The cat gave Andrew an enigmatic look from her amber eyes, yawned and wriggled herself into a more comfortable position.

'Leave her,' he smiled. 'She's beautiful. What's a few hairs between friends. She's part Persian, isn't she?' His fingers caressed the soft, cream fur.

The meal was perfect. Replete,

Andrew sat back in his chair and looked at her with admiration. 'You're some cook! No wonder you have so many regulars at the tearoom.'

'They appreciate good English food,' she said. 'They are mostly older people, I admit, but we do have quite a few younger ones at weekends.'

'Young people can't cook nowadays,' said Andrew. 'Not meals like that, anyway. Selena . . . '

She stopped him with a look. Collecting plates together, she carried them into the kitchen.

He jumped up and followed her. 'Poppy, I was only going to say that Selena can't cook. Hates it.'

She turned from plunging dishes into a bowl of soapy water, to face him. 'Please, Andrew, could we not talk about Selena.' She returned to the table and collected some more dishes.

When she came back, he was looking round the kitchen. 'No dishwasher?'

'I don't mind washing dishes,' she said, 'and usually there's only me. I use

44

the dishwasher at work, so this makes a change.'

He picked up a tea towel and began, awkwardly, to dry a plate. She laughed. 'It's plain you don't dry dishes very often.'

Her laughter lightened the atmosphere. Selena was forgotten and they worked in harmony until the last dish was dried and put away.

Back in the sitting-room with Mrs Beaton once more on his lap, Andrew looked at Poppy. 'Are you happy?'

'Happy? Do you mean now?'

'I think you are now,' he said, gently. 'No, I meant every day, in your life.'

'Is anyone happy every day?' She looked into the fire. 'I think I'm as happy as anyone has the right to be. I have my tearoom and my friends.'

'But no-one special? I'm sorry, I shouldn't have asked that.' He reached across Mrs Beaton to put his coffee cup on the little table.

'I've had my moments, of course,' Poppy tried to keep the conversation light, 'but no-one special.'

'And you've no idea of moving on to larger premises, a more prestigious place? The tearoom is quite small.'

'It's what I've always wanted. It has the sort of old-fashioned ambiance I love. And so do my customers, fortunately.' She picked up the coffee pot and replenished their cups. 'How's Jim? You've seen him today?'

'Not today. Last night, as you did. He's doing quite well, but fretting about his plants, as you might imagine.' Andrew finished his coffee. 'He thinks the world of you.'

Poppy smiled. 'We're great friends. We have the same ideas; growth and success in business, but slowly and quietly. We wouldn't get far in London, would we?'

'London.' Andrew looked into the fire. 'It seems so far away.'

Was he thinking about Selena, Poppy wondered.

'I sometimes wonder what I was doing there. This place is beginning to suit me very well.'

She was just going to ask whether that meant he might not go back to the city, when he looked at his watch.

'Excuse me,' he said to Mrs Beaton, and gently tipped her on to the floor. She gave an indignant yowl and stalked out of the room. Andrew stood up.

'It's been a lovely evening. Thank you so much.'

They walked to the front door. Poppy opened it and leaned back against the doorpost. Andrew looked at her, his eyes enigmatic. Then he bent and gave her a light kiss on the cheek. 'See you tomorrow.'

The light of the full moon shone brightly on his car. He opened the door and waved before climbing in. She watched him drive away, closed the door and gently touched the spot where his lips had briefly lingered.

3

Poppy loved candles. They were her one big extravagance. Two days later, on her return from work, she decided to have a leisurely bath and an early night with a book.

She ran the bath water, recklessly added a large measure of bath oil and lit six vanilla candles round the room. She switched off the overhead light and went downstairs for a glass of wine.

She was about to climb the stairs carrying the wine, when the phone rang. Glaring at it, she continued up the stairs.

But what if it's Jim? She turned and hurried back downstairs.

'Fancy a Chinese tonight?' asked a voice with a faint Scottish accent. Her heart sank. Ian Logan.

'It's rather short notice,' she replied.

'That's never bothered you before.'

'I know but . . . ' She sought inspiration and found none. 'It's just that I'm tired,' she said, lamely. 'I was going to have a bath and an early night.'

'But you have to eat,' Ian objected. 'If you're tired, a Chinese will save you the bother of cooking. I could bring a takeaway. We needn't go out.'

Poppy hesitated. Ian could argue for England, or in his case, Scotland. If she didn't give in, she'd be here all night. But she didn't want him to spend the evening in her house.

'Very well, Ian. Give me an hour then come and collect me. We'll go out. Thank you.' She replaced the telephone before he could say anything else.

She hurried into the bathroom, switched on the light and blew out the candles. It would have to be an in-and-out bath. Pity. She'd been looking forward to her early night.

Ian was on time, and an hour later, they were speeding towards the Jade Palace in his scruffy little blue car.

Poppy glanced at her companion out

49

of the corner of her eye. His hair was
longer than usual and he had the
beginnings of a beard. His position as
drama teacher at the local secondary
school gave him a certain licence as to
his appearance, but tonight he looked
even more Bohemian than usual. Also,
he seemed to be containing himself
with difficulty. There was an air of
suppressed excitement about him.

When Poppy had told Andrew there
was no-one in her life, she had
deliberately not mentioned Ian Logan.

For one thing, she didn't look on him
as someone special; for another, there
was no understanding between them.

On her part, he was just a friend,
someone to go out with occasionally.
His feelings were somewhat different.
He had proposed twice and showed
every sign of intending to do so at
intervals until she said yes. He was sure
he would wear her down in the end.

They entered the joss stick scented
restaurant and were bowed to a table. A
beautiful Chinese girl brought them

gold embossed menus and warm napkins and lit the candles on their table.

Despite her protests at changing her menus to incorporate foreign food, Poppy was quite fond of Chinese dishes.

'You can order,' she told Ian, 'but don't forget I like chicken in lemon sauce and duck in plum sauce.'

'That doesn't leave me much scope,' he pretended to grumble, but soon they were sitting back sipping drinks and looking at each other.

'I hear Andy Mabey is back,' said Ian. 'Is it permanent?'

'Possibly not,' said Poppy carelessly.

He looked at her levelly. 'You two used to be quite close, didn't you?'

She replaced the glass on the table. 'That was a long time ago. He has a girlfriend, Selena, now. Very metropolitan and sophisticated.'

He continued to look at her. 'So you're not interested?'

'In Andy. Good Heavens!'

'Is that a yes or a no?'

'Why? Is it important?'

'It is to me.' He reached into a pocket and brought out a small back box. He flicked it open and Poppy gasped at the lovely ring inside. It was designed as a pearl and garnet flower and was exquisite.

'A bit old-fashioned, like you,' said Ian, 'in the nicest possible way. Darling Poppy, will you marry me?'

Poppy looked at him and sighed. 'This is the third — no, the fourth time you've asked me.'

'Will you say yes?'

'I can't. I don't love you.'

Ian looked down at the ring. Poppy followed his gaze.

'I'd like to say yes if only for that beautiful ring,' she joked, 'but it wouldn't be right. I don't love you and I'm sure you don't really love me.'

Ian looked at her intently. 'You're wrong there. I do love you. And I won't stop asking you. One day you'll say yes.' He put the ring away in his pocket and looked up as the waitress appeared. 'Good! Food! I'm starving.'

Poppy smiled as she helped herself from the selection in front of her. He was easily distracted. 'Did you have a nice holiday?' she asked.

'It wasn't just a holiday,' said Ian, mysteriously. 'It was more than that. But I can't tell you now.'

He is in a peculiar mood tonight, thought Poppy, but I can't be bothered to ask questions. I'm too tired. She applied herself to the food.

Ian took her home as soon as they had finished the meal.

'Heavy day tomorrow,' he said. 'Auditions for the annual production. We're doing *Peter Pan* this year. I'll phone as soon as I get a free evening.'

Poppy allowed him two kisses but released herself as soon as she could. Ian Logan was quite interesting, a good friend, but he wasn't Andy Mabey.

★ ★ ★

Selena remained in London and Jim in hospital. Life went on peacefully; Poppy in her tearoom, Andy surrounded by plants and trees.

They met infrequently. One day, he popped in for a cup of coffee, bringing a rep with his catalogues, both talking business intently. Another, he waved to her from the office door as she arrived. But the evening at the cottage wasn't mentioned and wasn't repeated.

It's a week ago now, Poppy thought. He's forgotten all about it. But she was content to wait.

Ella arrived one morning with a serious face. 'Have we time for a chat?' she asked.

'Of course. You're early. We can spare ten minutes. I'll make us a drink.'

She glanced at her friend as she busied herself with the mugs and kettle. Ella's normally cheerful face was serious and her fingers fiddled nervously with a teaspoon.

Poppy placed the two mugs on the table.

'Poppy, when Andrew came to your cottage for a meal, did he mention his ideas for the tearoom?'

'Ideas? No. We talked about it for a little but nothing serious. Why?'

Ella glanced out of the window. 'Andrew and Chris went out for a drink last night. Andrew said he had plans for the tearoom.'

'Plans! What plans?' Poppy's voice was indignant.

'He thinks he could go up-market. He wants to change it to a French style restaurant.'

Poppy looked at her in horror.

'He thinks it should open for coffee in the morning and then dinner at night with a French menu,' Ella went on unhappily.

There was silence as the girls looked at each other, then Poppy spoke. 'That would change the character of the place completely. Are you sure Chris got it right?'

'He was perfectly clear about what Andrew had said.'

Andrew was in the office saying goodbye to the burly Dutch lorry driver. He smiled at Poppy as she entered, but the smile disappeared at her opening words.

'What's all this about turning my tearoom into a French restaurant?'

'Your tearoom?' Andrew gave her a quizzical look.

Poppy sat down facing him across the desk. 'Why do I have to learn this third hand? Couldn't you have mentioned it when we had dinner?'

'And spoiled a pleasant evening? Anyway, nothing is settled. It's just an idea.'

A sudden thought struck Poppy. 'Is it your idea — or Selena's? She was full of bright ideas when she was here.'

'Shall we discuss it when you're calmer?'

'I'm calm enough to discuss the destruction of all the plans I've made.'

'Poppy.' Andrew came round the desk and perched on the corner, looking down at her. 'Your tearoom is charming, popular, restful — and old-fashioned.'

'That's how my customers like it. You can't deny I'm doing well.'

'But you could do better. Old-fashioned is the key word. We should move with the times, get up to date. There isn't a French restaurant for a hundred miles. Let's create something that will appeal to a new young clientele with money to spend and an appreciation of an interesting menu. I'm not asking you to leave, just to change.' He bent forward and took her hand.

She snatched it away and stood up. 'And what about my customers, or clientele, if you prefer? Your grandmother is one of them,' she reminded him. 'She'll have something to say. It's a dreadful idea and I don't intend to discuss it — not until I've spoken to Jim.' Before Andrew could reply, she flounced out.

The tearoom was full when she returned. She made a rueful face at Ella, washed her hands and began to complete the orders.

For the next hour, they worked. Annoushka flew in and out with trays of food and Poppy and Ella toasted and buttered and grilled. When the last customer had been served, Poppy sat down, reached for some toast and buttered furiously.

'That Andy,' she muttered.

Ella poured two coffees and joined her at the table. 'You saw him?'

Poppy nodded. 'Chris was right.'

Ella took some toast and buttered it in silence. Then she asked, 'What are you going to do?'

'Speak to Jim,' said Poppy.

'Won't he side with Andrew?'

'Perhaps.' Poppy picked up her coffee cup. 'He's always been happy with my ideas, but now . . . ' She shrugged, 'Who knows.'

'I can't do French food,' said Ella. She had never attended a catering college. Poppy had taught her to cook so her knowledge was basic.

Poppy stood up. 'I think I'll conduct

an opinion poll.'

Many of Poppy's regular patrons came from St George's Court retirement flats, a large Georgian house ten minutes walk away. Andrew's grandmother, Mrs Sylvia Mabey, a sprightly widow in her seventies lived there and often came to lunch with her friend, Mr Bevington Wood.

They made a striking couple; Mrs Mabey in perfectly matched clothes and elegant silver hair, Mr Bevington Wood with his highly polished shoes and neatly trimmed goatee beard.

They were the acknowledged social leaders at St George's Court and usually occupied the centre table at Poppy's Tearoom. At tables nearby sat the other residents who either wanted to be seen in the right place or genuinely loved Poppy's cooking.

Today, the room was full, with practically every seat taken. Poppy looked round with satisfaction. It would be a good opinion poll.

Mrs Mabey and Mr Bevington Wood

had just finished their meal when Poppy approached. 'Would you like coffee?'

They said they would, and Poppy, after signalling through the serving hatch to Ella, returned to the table. 'May I speak to you for a few minutes?' she asked, and sat down, placing her clipboard in front of her. They looked at it with interest.

'You had the roast beef and Yorkshire pudding today, didn't you?' she asked.

'And very good it was, as usual,' said Mr Bevington Wood.

'Might you have preferred Coq au Vin?'

The two friends looked at each other and shook their heads.

'On holiday, yes, but here, no,' said Mrs Mabey. 'We enjoy your lovely English cooking.'

'And the apple tart and cream melted in the mouth.' Mr Bevington Wood laughed. 'I was almost tempted to order another slice.'

'So you would not have preferred

tarte tatin or crème brulée?'

'What's all this about?' asked the elderly man. 'I hope you're not going to mess about with the menu, young lady. There'll be some complaints if you do.'

Poppy folded her arms on the clipboard and leaned towards them. 'Your grandson,' she looked towards Mrs Mabey, 'has been having a re-think about the tearoom. He has some idea of changing it into a French restaurant. I wanted your opinion.'

Mr Bevington Wood's face was turning a shade of scarlet. 'The young puppy! What does his father say?'

'I don't think he knows,' said Poppy. 'It's just an idea at present.'

'It's a bad idea. He can forget all about it.'

'Don't worry about Andrew.' Mrs Mabey patted Poppy's arm. 'He'll be back off to London in a few months. He's just flexing his muscles, pretending he's the boss. Jim will sort him out when he comes home from hospital.'

'But what if he's right. Maybe people

would like the idea.' Poppy looked worried. 'I need to ask as many people as I can, then if Andrew tries to go ahead, I'll have some research to back up my argument.'

'Leave it to me,' said the elderly man, and stood up. He rapped on the sugar basin with his spoon. Gradually the laughter and chatter died away. All eyes turned to the imposing figure in the centre of the room.

'Ladies and gentlemen,' he began. Years ago he had been an actor, not a star, but well-known and he still retained the sonorous voice of his acting days. 'Our young friend here,' he indicated Poppy, 'has a problem.'

Fluently, he outlined Andrew's plans. There were a few appalled faces.

'Now I'm sure you agree with me that we don't want a French restaurant in place of our lovely tearoom.' There was a burst of applause. He lifted his hand for silence. 'Tonight, in the lounge at St George's Court, there will be a meeting to discuss the idea. Everyone is

welcome. Please come along at nine.'
He sat down to applause.

Poppy looked at him admiringly.
'Thank you, Mr Bevington Wood.'

'Don't thank me, young lady. I shall
enjoy it. Gives me something to do. A
project. We'll go home now,' he turned
to Mrs Mabey, 'and begin to draw up
some plans. French restaurant, indeed.'

4

When Poppy arrived at work the next morning, she found a small crowd battling against the wind to fasten a large banner to the gate. It read, SAVE POPPY'S TEAROOM.

Mr Bevington Wood was directing operations. He stood aside to let Poppy drive in and followed her to the carpark.

Poppy got out of her car. 'You had your meeting then?'

'Great success. You'd have been touched to hear what people said about you. So many came, not just from St George's Court but from the village and farther afield.'

Chris arrived with Ella. He didn't look pleased. 'What's all this? Andrew will be furious.'

'Not as furious as we are,' said the elderly man. 'This will show him what we think of his London ideas.'

Chris gave Ella a kiss and stalked off without another word. Ella looked at Poppy, raised her eyes and vanished into the tearoom.

'What else have you planned?' asked Poppy, curiously.

'You'll see.' Mr Bevington Wood went off towards the group and the gate.

A succession of people came in for coffee during the morning, but when Poppy tried to question them about the activities outside, they just smiled and put fingers to their lips.

At eleven, there was a lot of commotion at the gate. Several large vans arrived and equipment and cables were unloaded. Men were shouting orders and the protestors were moved to the side.

'Creep down and see what's going on,' said Poppy.

Ella was happy to do so. Poppy was amused to see her dart from bush to shed to greenhouse down the drive to the gate. She was soon back, bursting with excitement.

'There's a TV unit and a group of people from local radio. Mr Bevington Wood has organised it. He has contacts, they said.'

Poppy put her hands over her face. 'Just wait till Andrew gets here.' The two girls giggled nervously.

Mr Bevington Wood appeared, a pleased expression on his face. 'Would you come down and be interviewed, Miss Poppy?' he asked. 'I think you should put your point of view.'

Poppy was aghast. 'Oh no, Mr Bevington Wood. I couldn't possibly. Don't ask me. I'm sure you're doing fine without me.'

He looked doubtful. 'It would look better if you came.'

Poppy moved to put a table between herself and the excited man, as if he would drag her off forcibly.

'Look!' shouted Ella from the doorway. 'Andrew has arrived. There's his red car.'

Mr Bevington Wood hurried out and

Poppy joined Ella in the doorway. Ella took one look at her and darted off after the elderly man.

Poppy went back into the kitchen and sat at the table. This was getting out of hand. She'd only intended to do some simple market research and the idea had escalated into a full scale protest.

Ella rushed back out of breath. 'They marched round and round his car waving flags that said, SAVE POPPY'S TEAROOM and ENGLISH FOOD FOREVER. Mrs Mabey was in the thick of it. She's been interviewed by the local radio and Mr Bevington Wood and the others will be on TV tonight.'

'And what about Andrew?' asked Poppy.

'He turned the same colour as his car. When they questioned him, he refused to say anything. He couldn't get through the crowd so he's driven off down the road.'

That night, Poppy went to the hospital to visit Jim.

'I watched the early evening news on the television,' he said as she sat down. 'You've had a bit of excitement today, haven't you?'

Poppy gave him a worried look. She'd hoped to speak to him before he heard about the protest. But to her surprise, he seemed highly amused.

'I'm sorry,' he said. 'I know it's serious, but it was so funny to see Mr Bevington Wood organising his troops and then Andrew driving off with a face like thunder, and all because of our little tearoom.' He began to laugh and Poppy joined in. 'It's done me the power of good,' he said. 'What did Andy say when he came back?'

'I haven't seen him. The TV people left and the protesters melted away and everything went quiet.'

'Was the idea of a French café, Andy's or someone else's?' Jim asked.

Poppy looked at him. 'What do you think?'

'The same as you, I expect. I think it was Selena's idea. But she's not here now, so why does he bother?'

'Perhaps he too thinks it a good idea.'

'As soon as I get out of here,' said Jim, 'I'll be back in control. He knows that, so why embark on large scale projects? I asked him to keep things ticking over for me, not to make alterations and upset my friends.' He took Poppy's hand in his large rough one. 'Don't worry, Poppy, I won't let him make you unhappy.'

Tears sprang to her eyes as she looked at the man who had been her friend and supporter for so many years.

'You know, I once thought you and Andrew would make a go of things,' he said.

The tears vanished and a smile broke over her face. 'Andrew and I? You mean, get married?'

'Yes. You seemed very close at one time.'

'We were friends, close friends, but he would never think of me like that. He was always ambitious. He wanted a smart, go-ahead girl like . . . '

'Like Selena,' he finished for her. 'And has she made him happy? No. You're the one for him.'

'Jim!' Poppy stood up. 'Please don't say that to Andy. I'm in enough trouble with him as it is.' She bent and kissed his cheek. 'Now I really must go.'

Driving home, she thought of Jim's remark. She and Andrew married! What an idea! she smiled to herself. Yes, what an idea.

* * *

Poppy slept badly that night. Images of an irate Andrew kept intruding into her dreams and waking her up. When at last, her bedside clock said six, she decided to get up.

She decided to go to the garden centre earlier than usual. If she and Andy were to have a row, at least there would be fewer people to hear them.

As she turned into the gate, Andrew was parking his car on the far side of the carpark. She pretended not to notice him and hurried to get indoors.

She had just removed her coat when she heard a knock on the kitchen door. She took several deep breaths then called, 'Come in.'

'I thought I'd scrounge a coffee rather than make my own,' he said, as he came in and closed the door.

'Of course.' Poppy turned away and switched on the machine, busying herself with the coffee grinder. The chair legs screeched as he pulled out the chair and sat down at the table.

'Andrew. About yesterday.'

He held up a hand. 'Let's forget it. I was mad at the time but Gran phoned me last night and put me in the picture. It wasn't strictly your fault. It was taken out of your hands. And Mr Bevington Wood got carried away.'

Poppy said nothing.

'One person found it funny anyway,' he said.

'Your father?'

'My father. He was still chuckling when I saw him quite late last night. By

71

the way, the doctor wants to see me this morning. I'll go to the hospital as soon as Chris gets here.'

'Did the doctor say why he wanted to see you?'

'No. He'll explain when I get there. Can't be anything wrong; Dad seems so much better.'

Andrew had gone when Ella arrived, full of excited talk about the new baby who'd arrived next door in the middle of the night. She noticed the two mugs and stopped in mid-flow. 'Visitors?' she asked.

Poppy explained.

'So you and Andrew have made it up,' said Ella.

'He wants to forget it. He doesn't seem too upset.'

'How do you feel?'

'I can't help wondering that perhaps I should look for new premises. Start again somewhere else. After all, it is his tearoom at the moment.'

Ella looked at her in horror. 'Poppy, you can't. Think of the protesters and all the trouble they took to support you. It's not like you to give in so easily.'

Poppy smiled at her. 'You're right, of course. I can't let them down. If he starts talking about a French restaurant again, I'll come at him with all guns blazing.'

★   ★   ★

Andrew returned after lunch. He chose a table in a corner and when Poppy came to ask him what he would like to eat, he shook his head and motioned her to a chair beside him.

'I've just come from the hospital. Dr Wilson is very pleased with Dad. In fact, he says Dad can leave on one condition.'

'Which is?'

'That he spends the next few weeks in convalescence. You know Dad, he thinks he can come straight back here and pick up a trowel. Dr Wilson says if he doesn't agree to convalescence he'll have to stay in hospital.'

'So what has been decided?' asked Poppy.

'I phoned Pauline,' said Andrew. 'She'll be glad to have him for a few weeks.'

Andrew's sister, Pauline, was a few years older than them and married to a hotelier in a seaside resort not far away.

'What a good idea,' Poppy exclaimed. 'Pauline will look after him and he'll have sea air to build him up.'

'Exactly. Luckily he seems pleased with the idea.'

'What about Annie?'

'Annie?'

'Yes. Will she want to be with him?'

'She can't go because of the twins. They can't miss school.'

'What a shame. I'm sure she'd want to be there to look after him.'

Andrew smiled. 'Much as I love my stepmother, I'm not blind to her little, shall we say, weaknesses. Annie would prefer to let Pauline nurse him and welcome him back fit and well.'

'When will he go. You'll take him, of course?'

'I'll run him down on Monday. I was wondering . . . Monday is your day to be closed, so perhaps you'd like to come with us.'

'I'd like that very much,' said Poppy. 'What time shall we leave?'

'Nine o'clock from the hospital will be early enough. I'll ask Annie to pack his suitcase the night before.' Andrew still looked thoughtful.

'Is there another problem. You look concerned?'

Andrew sighed. 'Dr Wilson says that if Dad doesn't take it easy for another six months he'll need to retire, give up work altogether.'

'And that would mean . . . ?'

'Selling the business, or . . . ' he looked levelly at Poppy. 'I'd have to take over, stay here for good, give up my career in London.'

They sat in silence, each thinking of the implications of that statement. Then Poppy stood up.

'I must get back to work. Thank you for the invitation for Monday.'

'Thank you for accepting. We'll have a lovely day. By the way, this is for you.' He reached down and picked up a plant in a pot from beside his chair.

Poppy took the deep orange rose with its velvet petals and looked at him over the top.

'Thank you, it's beautiful.'

'Just like you,' said Andrew, softly.

5

With Jim settled comfortably under rugs in the back seat, Poppy prepared to enjoy the ride to the coast. Andrew was a fast driver, but careful, and she felt quite safe with him.

'You won't be really happy till you get back to your plants,' said Poppy.

'Won't be long,' growled Jim with satisfaction.

'If you don't do exactly as Pauline says; rest, eat and take gentle exercise, it will be long.'

Jim glared at the back of Andrew's head. 'Have I swapped one prison for another?'

'Of course not, but Pauline has had instructions from the doctor.'

'You promised to be good,' coaxed Poppy.

Jim sighed. 'I know. I'll be a model convalescent. I don't want to go back to hospital.'

Countryside gave way to houses, scattered at first, then becoming streets on the edge of the seaside town of Porthaven.

In no time, they drew up in front of the White Towers Hotel, a large gleaming white building facing the sea.

Pauline was an older version of Andrew, with the same wide smile and wide shoulders. Poppy had known her slightly when they were younger and remembered her as a jolly girl, always laughing. Pauline enveloped her brother in a bear hug then turned to Poppy.

'I remember you,' she smiled. 'Little Poppy Frane. You haven't changed a bit.' She gave the younger girl a hug too. 'Still with Andrew, eh?' She gave him a roguish dig in the ribs.

'Help me get Dad out,' said Andrew, ignoring her jollity. 'He'll be stiff after the ride.'

They were soon inside the hotel and seated in squashy, leather armchairs in the comfortable lounge.'

'What a lovely room.' Poppy looked

around admiringly.

'We seldom sit in here,' Pauline admitted. 'It's for the guests. But at this time on a fine day, it's usually empty. Now then, coffee everyone?'

'We'd love some coffee,' Andrew said, 'but then I want to take Poppy for a walk. She hasn't enjoyed any sea air for a long time.'

Pauline gave him one of her wicked smiles. 'We quite understand,' she said.

Poppy was beginning to feel just a little uncomfortable when the entry of a dark-haired, stocky man captured Pauline's attention.

'Marco, at last! Come over and say hello to your long lost relatives. We're so busy we haven't seen the family for over a year,' she explained to Poppy.

Marco had the expansive smile of his wife. He shook hands with Jim and Andrew then turned to Poppy.

'And who is this charming young lady?' He lifted her hand to his lips and gazed at her with his deep chocolate eyes. Poppy blushed.

'Now then, Marco, you old roué, leave her alone. She belongs to Andrew.'

Poppy caught Andrew's eye and he gave a resigned shrug. 'I think Poppy and I will go for our walk,' he said, getting to his feet and holding out a hand to Poppy. 'What time would you like us back?' he asked Pauline.

'Marco is going to cook you a beautiful Italian meal,' said Pauline. 'Mind you are back by one.'

They set off down the steps in front of the hotel and Andrew took her arm to cross the road.

'A beautiful Italian meal,' he murmured. 'Shall you mind that?'

'Of course not,' Poppy retorted, 'I love Italian food.'

Andrew gave her a quizzical smile.

'Just because I want my café to be traditionally English doesn't mean I can't enjoy other cuisine,' she replied with dignity.

The tide was out and they strolled slowly along the wide expanse of sand.

Seabirds swooped from the promenade to the water's edge; a soft wind whipped Poppy's hair across her face; she breathed in the salty air and lifted her face to the sun.

Andrew smiled at her pleasure. He bent and picked up a white shell with a pearly pink inside. 'A gift from Porthaven,' he said, presenting it to Poppy. She studied it and put it carefully in her jacket pocket. Then she bent, picked up an identical one and gave it to Andrew.

'A present for you,' she said, gravely.

They strolled on. Andrew tucked her hand under his arm. Poppy felt herself relax. She was happy. For now, Selena didn't exist.

The meal with Andrew's family was a noisy, happy occasion. Pauline and Marco had infectious laughs and Poppy found herself joining in the jokes and the banter.

Pauline and Marco's two children, Petra and Paul, had joined them for lunch; teenagers, but with none of the shyness of some young people. They seemed genuinely pleased to see Poppy and Andrew.

'This is a wonderful pasta,' Poppy said to Marco. He kissed his fingers to her.

'Fusilli Puttanesca. Pasta with a special sauce of olives, tomatoes and capers. My mama taught me to cook. She is the best cook in all Italia.'

When they had finished eating, Pauline led the way to the pretty garden at the back of the hotel where coffee was set out on a table under the trees.

'You'll do very well if you eat like this and rest in this garden every day,' Poppy told Jim, who was looking around critically.

'I can see a few things that need attention,' he muttered, 'and that border could do with thinning out.'

'You're here to rest,' Andrew reminded him.

Pauline overheard the remark. 'I'll watch him. You'll have him back as good as new in a few weeks.'

Poppy lay back in a reclining chair and listened to the chatter flowing to and fro around her. She felt so comfortable with Andrew's family. She glanced across at him and he caught the look and smiled back as if he knew what she was thinking.

'You are in love with Andrew?' a soft voice asked and Poppy found that Petra had slipped into the seat next to her.

'Oh . . . I . . . ' She was flustered and unsure what to answer, but the girl went on, 'because he is in love with you. I have seen how he looks at you.'

'No. I don't think so.' Poppy had regained her composure and was afraid Andrew could hear their conversation. 'We are just old friends. He has a girlfriend in London,' she said, quietly.

'I know I am right,' said Petra, with conviction. 'You will see.'

Andrew stood up. 'I'm sorry to leave this comfortable party, but Poppy and I must be getting back. We have work tomorrow.' He smiled at Poppy who got to her feet and looked for her bag and jacket.

Goodbyes and thanks and invitations to come again took up the next fifteen minutes, but at last, she was alone with Andrew and heading away from Porthaven towards home. She stifled a yawn and snuggled back comfortably into her seat.

'Tired?' Andrew looked at her with concern.

'Comfortably so. Sea air and good food. I could just drift off to sleep.'

He looked disappointed. 'Go to sleep then. I'll wake you when we get to your house.'

Poppy lowered the car window and took a few deep breaths. Time on her own with Andrew was too precious to waste on sleeping. She closed the window and gave him a bright smile.

'There, I'm awake now.'

He put a hand on her knee and gave it a squeeze. 'Good. We can talk.'

She waited expectantly. He said

nothing but concentrated on the road ahead.

'Did you . . . did you want to talk about anything special?' she asked, tentatively.

'No. Nothing special. But if I don't have some chat to keep me awake, I might go to sleep. I've had sea air and good food too, don't forget.'

Poppy hid her disappointment. She wasn't sure what she wanted Andrew to talk about, unless it was their relationship. What relationship? she asked herself.

'Did you remember Pauline?' he asked. 'She married Marco soon after you began to help at Bramleys, and moved away.'

'I remember her laugh,' said Poppy. 'She was always laughing.'

'I'm sorry about her silly remarks,' he said, with embarrassment.

'Silly remarks? Oh yes, of course.' Poppy remembered Pauline saying, 'She belongs to Andrew.' 'I didn't take any notice,' she lied.

85

They drove on for a few miles in silence.

'She was thinking of years ago,' Andrew said. 'We were very close then. Do you remember?'

Do I remember? Poppy couldn't trust herself to speak.

'It was quite a while ago.' Andrew misunderstood her silence. 'I'm sure you've had lots of boyfriends since then. I expect you forgot me as soon as I left for college.'

'I went away to college too,' she reminded him. 'My life changed.'

'We're different people now,' he said, 'with different experiences and different aims.'

Is he thinking about Selena, Poppy wondered. Why must that wretched girl come between us, even when she's not here?

She was relieved when, a few miles later, Andrew drove into the car park of a country pub. The conversation was getting difficult. She opened the car door and slid out into the welcome fresh air.

'Come on, we'll get a coffee, it will wake us up.' Andrew led the way to the door through which light spilled out on to the cobbles. 'Then in half an hour we should be home.'

★ ★ ★

'May we disrupt your tearoom and push a few tables together?' asked Mr Bevington Wood. 'We're having a bit of a celebration and we'd like to sit together.'

He turned and gestured towards the group of about ten people who'd accompanied him and Mrs Mabey into the café.

'What's all that about?' asked Ella.

'I'm not sure, but I have an idea,' said Poppy. 'Look at Mrs Mabey. She looks rather pleased with herself.'

'If they're settled now, I'll go and take their orders,' said Poppy a few minutes later.

Mrs Mabey fluttered the fingers of her left hand as Poppy approached. The solitaire diamond on her second finger flashed in the sunlight which streamed through the diamond panes of the window.

'She's accepted me at last,' said Mr Bevington Wood. 'This is our engagement party.'

'I was right,' said Poppy, returning to the kitchen. 'They're engaged.'

'How wonderful,' said Ella. 'I hope they're going to have their reception here.'

'They are. They've just asked me if the twenty-ninth is free.'

As the meal ended, Mr Bevington Wood stood up. 'Just a few words,' he said, completely ignoring the other diners in the room. 'Life is full of surprises. Not only am I to embark on a life of matrimony, but I intend to resume my career.'

There was a gasp of surprise.

'As a result of my appearance on television the other morning, I have been offered a part in a new serial which is to come out in the autumn.'

There was a round of applause.

'He's playing a tramp,' said Mrs Mabey.

Everyone laughed. The thought of the elegant Mr Bevington Wood as a tramp amused them all.

'A gentleman tramp,' he said with dignity. 'I always wear a tie.' He sat down to more applause.

Andrew appeared in the kitchen doorway.

'What's all the noise? Sounds like you've got a bunch of teenagers in there.'

'It's your grandma.' Ella began to explain.

'Don't say she didn't tell you?' Poppy was surprised.

'My dear grandmamma never tells me anything she plans to do. You should know that by now. And her friend, Mr Bevington Wood, is a bad influence on her,' he said, with a mock scowl. 'What have they been up to now? Not another demonstration, I hope.'

'You'd better go and see.' Poppy and

Ella were both laughing.

Andrew strode into the café and over to the table where everyone was having a wonderful time. The girls saw him lift his grandmother's hand and examine the ring. Then he bent and kissed her cheek and she patted his. Her fiancé stood up and shook Andrew's hand vigorously.

'Well that seems all right.' Poppy turned to load the dishwasher.

Mrs Mabey spotted Poppy in the kitchen doorway and beckoned her over.

'I was just telling Andrew that we'd booked the tearoom for the twenty-ninth for our wedding reception. It will be the perfect place,' she said, giving him a determined look, 'and we don't need a marquee.'

'You must come in some time and discuss the menu,' said Poppy hastily, before Andrew could speak.

Andrew smiled down at his grand-mother. 'If Poppy does it, it will be perfect. Now I must go. I have work to do.' He kissed his grandmother again and walked towards the kitchen followed by Poppy.

Ella was still rushing busily round the kitchen. Andrew gestured to Poppy and she followed him outside.

'I just wanted a few words with you,' he said. 'Have you recovered from your day at the seaside?'

'It was lovely,' she said. 'But I haven't had time to think about it. Mrs Mabey and Mr Bevington Wood came in this morning and it's been excitement ever since.'

He turned and gazed out over the plants and greenhouses of the garden centre. 'I did a lot of thinking when I got home last night,' he said. 'You know that if Dad doesn't come back, the choice will be between selling the business or . . . '

'You taking over,' she finished. 'Yes, I know.'

'A few weeks ago, I wouldn't have considered staying here. My life was in London. But now, I'm beginning to see things differently. I've almost decided that I want to stay here.' He turned to her and put his hands on her shoulders. 'What do you think, Poppy? Should I stay?' he looked down into her eyes and she felt her heart beat faster.

'I . . . I can't decide for you,' she stammered. 'You must do what you want to do.'

'But would you be glad if I stayed? You'd be here and I'd be over there, but we'd be working together again. Just like old times. What do you think?'

'If you want it, then I want it too,' she whispered.

6

Poppy woke the next morning with a feeling of elation. Sun through the slats of the blind threw a golden pattern on her quilt and Mrs Beaton was stretched out comfortably in the centre.

Poppy smiled and scratched the cat's soft ears. Why do I feel so content? she wondered. Then she remembered.

Of course. Andrew had said he might stay. They would work together as before. They would resume their friendship and who knew what might follow. Petra's forecast could come true.

She swung her legs from the bed, ran to the window and flung up the blind. A perfect late summer day. She opened the window and the fresh morning air came flooding in.

When Ella arrived Poppy had already laid all the tables in the tearoom and was drinking a glass of orange juice in the kitchen doorway.

'You look very fresh and newly minted,' said Ella. 'What's happened? Has Andrew proposed?'

'I haven't seen Andrew since he was here yesterday. Would you like some orange?'

'I'd love some.' Ella put on her apron. 'Why are you looking so pleased with yourself? I know, Ian Logan has proposed.'

'You've got a one-track mind,' said Poppy, pouring a glass of juice and handing it to her friend. 'Ian is always proposing. That would be nothing new.' She took a deep breath. 'It's a lovely day. I just feel good.'

Ella eyed her speculatively. 'Did Andrew have anything special to say when he lured you outside yesterday?'

Poppy had intended to keep their conversation to herself; now she couldn't help telling Ella.

'He's thinking of staying and running the garden centre. He's beginning to like being back in the country — the slower pace and so on. In fact, he doesn't want to go back to London.'

She finished on a triumphal note and gave Ella a wide smile. 'Oh Ella, I do hope he decides to stay.'

Poppy had just placed a tray on a corner table and was handing out the cups of coffee, when the little bell on the door tinkled, signalling new customers. Poppy, exchanging smiles with the ladies at the table, glanced up.

Two people had walked in, looked around the room and chosen a table. The woman was Selena.

Selena, in a deep pink coat and matching shoes, sat with a little smile playing about her lips.

'Good morning, Poppy,' said Selena, brightly. 'May I introduce my friend, Monsieur Henri Caron? Henri, this is Poppy, who runs the tearoom.' She gave him a meaningful look. 'Henri is from France,' she said, unnecessarily.

Poppy nodded to him but said nothing. The Frenchman stood up and took her hand. She wondered if he was going to kiss it, but he just held it a moment, murmured 'Mademoiselle Poppy,' then sat down again.

'Won't you join us for a little chat?' asked Selena.

'What should we chat about?' Poppy forced her voice not to waver.

'The tearoom,' said Selena, sweetly. 'Remember, before I went away, we discussed ideas for modernising it?'

'You had ideas,' said Poppy. 'We didn't discuss them. I wasn't interested.'

Selena's face coloured slightly with annoyance. She changed the subject.

'Have you seen Drew? I've been to the office but he wasn't there.'

'I've no idea where he is,' said Poppy. 'You'll have to ask one of his staff.' She began to walk away when a thought struck her. 'You mean, Andrew didn't know you were coming?'

'No. It was just a whim,' said Selena gaily. 'Henri and I were both free so we decided to drive down and surprise him.'

Poppy looked at her coldly. 'Someone will come and see if you want more coffee in a moment,' she said, and walked off before Selena could say any more.

Andrew arrived at the kitchen door ten minutes later. One of his gardeners had seen Selena in the office and told him.

'Poppy.' He took her hands. 'I didn't know she was coming. She gave me the impression she'd gone back for good.'

'She said you didn't know.' Poppy's voice was toneless.

'I'll have to speak to her.' Andrew sighed and walked into the tearoom.

Poppy leaned against the wall trembling. The one thing she had dreaded had happened. Selena had returned. Andrew would contrast the cool, immaculate city girl with the agitated country mouse. Which would he prefer? Which would any man prefer?

She bit her lip. Please don't let him be influenced by her ideas again, she prayed. And what about the Frenchman? He and Selena would make a forceful team. What could she do?

The other customers had left the café. Selena, Henri and Andrew were alone so they made no attempt to lower their voices.

'But Drew, you know it makes sense,' said Selena. 'I'm thinking of you and the future of Bramleys. Henri and I can help you with the conversion — do it for you, if you're too busy. Henri is very experienced. I think it's what you really want,' she said with a sly smile.

Andrew had not sat down at the table. Now he turned away, saying as he did so, 'We can't talk here. I'll be in the office at twelve-thirty. I'll take you both to lunch.' Without another word, he marched out of the door.

Poppy, watching through the serving hatch, saw Selena smile at Henri, the satisfied smile of a woman who is sure she'll get what she wants.

★ ★ ★

'What are you going to do this evening?' Ella asked, as they cleaned up after closing time.

'Nothing special,' Poppy replied, tonelessly. 'Sit at home and wonder what happened when Andrew took those two beauties out to lunch.'

'I thought so. Now I'll tell you what you're going to do. You'll come home with me. Chris will be a bit later tonight, so I'll tell him to call for a takeaway and a bottle of wine on his way home.'

Later that evening, stretched out on Ella's couch, a glass of wine in her hand, her thoughts began to drift. What had happened at the lunch? Had Andrew spent the rest of the day with Selena? Was he with her now?

Ella caught the look on her face. 'More wine?' she asked, jumping up and refilling Poppy's glass.

Poppy, recalled to the present, smiled at her friend. Bother Selena. Why should she spoil a nice evening thinking of her?

Later, Chris made coffee. As she drank it, Poppy looked around the little sitting-room, inexpensively furnished, but bright with the colourful tapestry work Ella loved to do.

Ella and Chris sat on the couch holding hands. Poppy smiled at them. It must be lovely to have someone with you every day to share your interests — and your problems.

Poppy had never been anxious to marry, perhaps the right man had never appeared, but now, seeing her friend's happiness, she wondered whether she was missing something.

Her thoughts had drifted back to Andrew and of course, Selena. Cross with herself, she stood up.

'It's been a lovely evening but I'd better go,' she said, reluctantly. 'We all have work tomorrow.'

The telephone woke her early. Grumbling, yet glad, because she was sleeping so soundly she might have overslept, she went downstairs to answer it. It was Ian. He sounded very cheery and wide awake.

'Sorry if woke you,' he said, 'but I'm on my way out. Have to be at school early today. I wondered whether you're free for dinner tonight.'

Poppy rubbed her eyes sleepily. 'Well, I suppose . . . '

'You're not doing anything else? Good. I'll pick you up at seven-thirty. There's something I want to discuss with you.'

When she'd replaced the phone and made her way into the kitchen to make a cup of tea, Poppy wondered why she'd given in so easily. She didn't want dinner with Ian, in fact, she didn't really want to see Ian again. There was only one person she wanted to have dinner with . . .

She wondered whether Andrew would come and tell her what had gone on between him and Selena and Henri. If she got to work early, he might come over and speak to her before anyone else arrived. She drank her tea quickly and went back upstairs to dress.

* ★ ★

There was no sign of Andrew when she arrived at the garden centre; no light in the office, no car in the car park. Disappointed, Poppy made herself some toast and ate it standing at the window watching for his arrival.

When Ella came in, Poppy had to abandon her post. And when the tearoom began to fill with customers, she was too busy even to think of Andrew.

Halfway through the morning, Chris appeared with a basket of glowing, red tomatoes. 'These are beautiful,' he said, 'I thought you might like some for your customers.'

Poppy thanked him and transferred the tomatoes to a china bowl. 'I haven't seen Andrew this morning.' She tried to sound unconcerned.

'He hasn't come in yet,' said Chris, turning to go.

Ella looked at Poppy.

'He's still with her,' said Poppy. 'I

know he is.' She bit her lip and took a deep breath.

Ella looked at her, then ran after Chris. They talked for a few moments then she came back, with a smile on her face.

'They've gone,' she said. 'Selena and the Frenchman. Back to London.'

'How does Chris know that if he hasn't seen Andrew this morning?'

'Andrew told him last night, before they left work. Perhaps he threw them out.' Ella gave a little giggle.

'But if Chris knew last night, why didn't he tell us?'

'Probably didn't think we'd want to know. Men aren't as keen on gossip as we are. Anyway, we weren't going to talk about her last night, were we?'

'No, and I won't talk about her now,' said Poppy. 'but I do wish Andrew would call in. If he would just tell us that things will go on as before.'

'He'll come,' said Ella, without much conviction. 'He'll know you want to talk to him.'

103

But there was no sign of Andrew for the rest of the day. The garden centre was so well-organised and the staff so hard-working, that it almost ran itself.

When Ella and Annoushka had gone, Poppy made herself a cup of coffee and carefully locked all the doors and windows. Then she drew the curtains in the kitchen and settled with her account books at the table. She worked solidly for an hour; adding up rows of numbers, making lists and comparing profits each week. At last she sat back, stretching her arms above her head.

'Satisfactory,' she muttered. 'No, more than satisfactory.' If the business continued like this, she and Jim would soon be having that important talk.

A soft knock at the kitchen door made her jump. Andrew! She got up hurriedly and rushed to the door. But with her hand on the lock, she paused. What if it wasn't Andrew.

'Who is it?' she called.

'Ian.'

She unlocked the door and he came

in, grabbing her by the shoulders and planting a kiss on her cheek. He'd aimed for her lips but she'd turned her head slightly and he missed. It didn't seem to bother him very much, he was obviously bursting with excitement.

'I've been dying to talk to you all day but I couldn't get away,' he said. 'I couldn't wait until seven-thirty.'

'How did you know I was still here?'

'I went to your house and when you weren't in, I guessed you were still here.'

'Would you like a drink while you tell me whatever it is?'

'It's too exciting for that. We're going out to dinner. I'll tell you then.'

'I've been doing the books. I'm tired. I won't be good company,' she protested.

'Have you eaten?'

'No,' she admitted.

'Very well,' he said, as if that settled it. 'We'll go to the Raven. Pub meal. You needn't dress up, so there's no need to go home.'

She slipped a soft suede jacket over her shoulders and picked up her handbag. 'I'm ready.'

★ ★ ★

The bar of the Raven was large and divided into individual areas by screens of mock-old wood. There were huge log fires, welcome at the cool end of summer, and pots and vases of red glass which glowed in the firelight. Poppy liked it best in the winter when it had the cosy air of a Christmas card inn.

Ian returned from the bar with a glass of beer for himself and a white wine for Poppy. He swung into the chair opposite and took a swig of his beer.

'Now then,' he began, 'remember when you asked me about my holiday and I said it was more than a holiday?'

She nodded and picked up her drink.

'It was a job interview,' he announced.

'You're leaving teaching?'

'Yes, sort of. I'm going into the theatre.'

'Acting? It's a very precarious profession,' she objected.

'I'm not going to be an actor. I'm going to help to run a children's theatre company based in the Highlands. They've been going for a few years so they're tried and tested. They have a base for the winter, a small theatre and they spend the summer touring.' His face was shining with enthusiasm. 'I heard this morning that I've got the job. I start after Christmas.' He flung himself back in the chair and gave her a wide, satisfied grin.

'Congratulations,' she said. 'Have you told them at school?'

'Yes. Had to give as much notice as possible to give them time to replace me.'

Their meals arrived and they began to eat. Enjoying it, Poppy was aware that Ian was studying her.

'You know what I want?' His voice was quiet.

The serious look on his face disturbed her.

'I want you to marry me and come and live in the Highlands with me.'

'The Highlands? You mean you want me to go and live in Scotland? But I don't know anybody in Scotland. All my friends are here. And what about my tearoom?'

'That's all right,' he said, triumphantly. 'They have a little café at the theatre. You can help to run that.'

She looked at him in amazement. 'Help to run a little café? It's not the same thing at all. You don't understand, do you?'

'Well' — he looked desperately around the bar — 'perhaps we could get you another place of your own.'

Poppy gave a deep sigh. 'Ian, thank you for the compliment, but I wish you'd understand. I don't love you and I don't want to leave my business. I wish you all the success in the world with your new venture, but I can't be part of it.'

Ian's shoulders slumped. 'I think I've know all along that you'd never accept me. I've just been making a fool of myself.'

'No, Ian.' There was distress in her voice and she took his hand across the table. 'Don't ever think that. I like you a lot, but that isn't enough for marriage. But we can still be friends. I'll come up to the Highlands for a holiday and you can show me around. It will be something to look forward to.'

She knew as she spoke that it would never happen. So did Ian, but he pretended too.

'That's a good idea. We mustn't lose touch.'

They drove to her house in silence. He stopped at the gate.

'Don't get out,' she urged him. 'Thank you for . . . ' she was going to say, 'a nice evening,' but it wasn't, especially for him. 'For a lovely meal,' she finished.

He was looking ahead, his hands patting the steering wheel. 'I can't pretend I'm not upset,' he said, 'but I have to be fair. You never promised anything.'

She looked at him, unsure what to say.

'I suppose it was always Andrew Mabey,' he said, bitterly, 'even when he was away.'

Poppy opened her door. 'Andrew has nothing to do with it. I've given you my reasons. Now I must go. Goodbye, Ian. Good luck.'

7

'Annie, would you mind if I popped over to see you?' Poppy had waited until the last customers had left the tearoom, before telephoning Jim's wife.

'Poppy! I'd love to see you. We haven't had a chat for ages. Can you come now?'

Leaving Ella and Annoushka to clear away the chaos of the day, Poppy tidied her face and hair and made for the big house on the far side of the garden centre.

It was really too large for two adults and two teenagers, who would soon be going away to college, but Jim and Annie loved it.

Poppy stopped at the edge of the ornamental pool in front of the house to smile at the antics of the pretty little fancy ducks which were Annie's pets.

'Poppy!' Annie had been watching for

her and hurried out of the door. 'What a lovely surprise. I was longing for a visitor.'

She took Poppy into the house, through the long black and white paved hall which led from the front to the back of the house, and out into the garden.

'I've laid tea under the trees. It won't be so hot there. The sun is quite bright even though it's the end of the afternoon.'

She settled Poppy into a cushion-filled basket chair and made off towards the house. 'Won't be a moment, the kettle has just boiled.' She was back very soon with a large teapot. 'Here we are. Now help yourself. You like scones and clotted cream, don't you? I know you like cream.'

Annie had a good, but unfashionable appetite, as her figure showed. She tucked into the scones, pressing them upon her guest, until Poppy had to protest.

'Annie, I shall pop if I eat any more.

But they're delicious. I shall have to get you to make them for the tearoom.' She sat back in her chair and picked up her cup and saucer. 'Have you heard from Jim recently?'

'He's very good. Pauline spoils him, but she's let him do a bit of gentle gardening, so he's happy.' Annie's cheerful face beamed at Poppy. 'I'm taking the twins down to see him on Saturday.'

'They'll enjoy that. Give Jim my love.'

They drank their tea in silence for a few minutes then Annie looked at her guest. 'Was there . . . I mean, did you want to talk to me about anything in particular?'

Poppy replaced her cup and saucer on the table. 'Andrew hasn't been to work for several days. Nobody has seen him. I wondered whether . . . whether you knew where he was.'

'Andrew? Hasn't been to work? But where is he?'

'That's what I hoped you could tell me.'

'Oh, of course. Silly me. I was just surprised. He's usually very reliable. So who's in charge? Chris?'

'Yes.'

'Doesn't he know where Andrew is?'

'He says he doesn't. I don't know whether to believe him. He seems very calm about being suddenly left in charge with no warning.'

Annie shook her head slowly. 'I can't think where he can be. He's not with his father, that's for sure. Jim would have said.'

'He lives here, doesn't he?'

'Yes, but he has his own rooms at the far end, and his own front door. He can come and go as he likes. We don't see him for days sometimes and I try not to interfere with his life.'

'So you wouldn't realise he wasn't around?'

Annie didn't answer; she appeared to be thinking. 'What about that girl,' she said at last. 'Selena. You know, the one who was here some time ago and went back to London.'

'She came back last week,' said Poppy, 'just for a day. That was the last time I saw Andrew. He took her out to lunch.'

'Where is she now? Has she disappeared?'

'Chris says she's gone back to London.'

'Well then, Andrew's gone too.' Annie's triumphant look vanished as she saw Poppy's expression. 'Oh, Poppy, I'm sorry, I should have remembered. You and Andrew were once . . .'

'That was a long time ago. Andrew isn't interested in me now.'

'But I think you are still interested in him,' said Annie, quietly.

'I've fought against it.' Poppy's lip began to quiver. 'I know he wants a very different sort of girl from me. But when we were younger . . .' Her voice began to shake and she steadied it with a determined effort. 'When we were younger,' she went on, 'we were so happy together. We had so many plans for the future, so many shared interests.

I always loved him,' she admitted, 'but when he went away, he changed. He forgot about me. He fell for girls like Selena.' The tears began to fall. 'I haven't got a chance.'

Annie handed her a tissue. The kind eyes in the plump face were concerned. She wished she could think of something to say. She put her hand on Poppy's and pressed gently.

Poppy wiped her eyes. 'And now he's disappeared and I'm sure you're right, he's back with Selena.'

'I'll make some more tea.' Annie believed a cup of tea to be the answer to all problems.

'No.' Poppy reached out and held her arm. 'Please don't bother. I must get back. I've left all the work for Ella and Annoushka.'

'I wish I could have been more help. Don't worry, Andrew's a big boy. No harm can come to him. But I'm afraid there's nothing you can do about Selena. If Andrew is sensible, he'll know where his future should lie.'

Mrs Mabey and two friends came for afternoon tea the next day. 'We're going to make plans,' said Mrs Mabey, gaily. 'Susan and Clare are going to help me. They're my bridesmaids.' The three elderly ladies went off into peals of laughter.

Poppy called Ella, who came running out with a notebook and pen.

'Ella is our wedding advisor,' said Poppy solemnly.

Ella flushed with pleasure. 'Have you chosen a colour theme,' she asked Mrs Mabey, 'for the flowers and tablecloths and so on.'

'I like lilac,' said Mrs Mabey pensively.

'That's half mourning,' squealed Susan.

'So it is. Well we don't want that,' said the bride to be.

'Yellow and white?' suggested Ella.

'Yellow and white sounds lovely. Now you're the expert. Can I leave it all to you?'

Ella looked pleased. She loved planning receptions.

After ten minutes, she returned to Poppy in the kitchen. 'They're like children,' she said, but her eyes were dancing. 'This is certainly going to be different from our usual weddings.'

★ ★ ★

The insistent ringing of the telephone startled Poppy into wakefulness. She clicked on the bedside lamp and peered at her little white clock. One-thirty! The telephone was still ringing. She raced downstairs and snatched it up.

'Hello. What is it?'

'Poppy! Quickly!' an agitated voice squealed down the line. 'We're on fire, or rather, your tearoom is.'

Poppy, now wide awake, shivered from cold and shock. 'Annie? Is that you?'

'Yes. I've phoned for the fire brigade. Get down here as soon as you can.' The telephone was slammed down.

Five minutes later, she turned into the car park of Bramleys. The dark night was lit up by flames coming out of the end of her building.

Firemen surrounded the fire engine and heaved long hoses between them to the blazing building. A stream of water was aimed at the flames. Poppy clapped her hands to her face. No! Not her lovely tearoom!

Annie appeared at her side and then Ella and Chris. Chris was muttering and cursing to himself. Ella, eyes streaming from the smoke, clutched Poppy's arm.

'Whatever can have happened?'

Poppy made no answer but stared in horror.

'They've got it under control,' Chris yelled above the noise of shouting and crackling and rushing water. 'It doesn't seem to be spreading any further.'

They watched as the flames shrank down and in places, went out. A fireman came over to them.

'You the owner?' he asked Chris.

Chris indicated Poppy.

'Lucky we got here so fast,' said the fireman. 'The end room — the kitchen, is it? — is ruined. But I think we've saved the rest with not too much damage.'

Poppy, feeling the acrid smoke in the back of her throat, was unable to thank him.

Annie's offer of coffee was gratefully received by the fire crew and she and Ella hurried off to her house, to return in ten minutes with trays of drinks. Poppy and Chris went to investigate the ruined building as soon as it was safe.

'What do you think could have caused it?' she asked.

A fireman standing nearby heard her question. 'Looks like arson to me, but you'll have to wait for a proper investigation.'

A police car arrived and Poppy answered questions in her croaky voice.

'We'll be round to see you in the morning,' said the policeman. 'You don't seem to have enough voice to talk now.'

In daylight, the next day, the extent of the damage could be seen. The kitchen was a wreck, but the rest of the café had escaped. Curtains and carpet had a stale smoke smell and would need cleaning, but liberal washes in soapy water would clean up walls and furniture.

The police came early and later, an investigator from the insurance company.

In the middle of the afternoon, Poppy heard a familiar welcome voice.

'I turn my back and what happens? You try to burn the place down.'

'Jim!' She dropped her cloth and ran across the room to fall into his arms. 'Oh Jim, I'm so glad you're back,' and for the first time since the fire started, she burst into tears.

'There, there, little one, I was only joking.' Jim patted her back with one big hand while the other held her close.

'But are you better?' she sniffed. 'Should you be here?'

'I'm quite better and it's more than

time I came back. Annie phoned me and I knew my place was here. Especially as that wretched son of mine seems to have disappeared.'

Poppy found she was glad Annie had told Jim everything. She blew her nose. 'We . . . we don't know where he is. Selena came and Andrew disappeared. I suppose he's gone with her.'

'Well don't let's bother about them. Come along, we'll go and inspect the damage and then start repairs.'

Jim's reappearance galvanised everyone. By the next morning, workmen were clearing rubble, building walls, glazing windows and installing new doors.

By the end of the week, Poppy and Ella had a gleaming new kitchen.

Police inquiries had failed to solve the question of who had started the fire, for it was generally acknowledged that it was arson.

Chris and Ella muttered together about Ian Logan. 'Poppy hasn't any enemies,' Ella said for the umpteenth time. 'Ian is the only person I can think

of who'd have a grudge against her.'
But without any proof, they decided to
say nothing to Jim or the police.

'We'll wait,' said Chris. 'Some proof
might come up. Not that I can believe it
of Ian.'

'Poppy, could I come and see you
after work? It's important. I want you to
meet someone.'

Poppy looked at the telephone in her
hand in surprise. Ian Logan! Surely
they'd parted for good.

'Well, I don't know . . . ' she began.

'It's important, Poppy,' he said again.
'It's not about us. We won't stay long.
And if you could get Andy or Chris, it
would be useful.'

By now, Poppy was intrigued. What
could Ian be on about?

'Very well, Ian, if it won't take long.
I'll see Chris in a moment.'

'About six, then.' Ian replaced the
phone before she could change her
mind.

Poppy dialled the office number and
relayed Ian's request. Chris promised to

be with her at six. 'Didn't he say what it was all about?'

'No. Just that it was important.'

'It had better be,' growled Chris.

By six o'clock, Poppy and Chris were waiting in a tidied tearoom. As she glanced at her watch, there was a knock at the door. Chris motioned her to stay where she was and went to open it.

Ian Logan ushered in a small, worried looking woman, a tall stern man and two teenagers. Poppy recognised them at once.

'Aren't you the boys who . . . ?'

'The boys who caused a disturbance here one afternoon,' said Ian. 'Yes. Michael and David Goodall. This is Mr and Mrs Goodall.'

They stood around in an embarrassed group until Ian asked if they could all sit down. Poppy quickly indicated a table and they were soon seated, looking at Ian in various stages of expectancy.

'I have a little office off the gym at school,' he began. 'Yesterday, I was in there writing up some notes when a group of boys came into the gym and began to tidy the PE cupboards. They obviously didn't know I was there.

'After a while their conversation seemed to intrude on my thoughts and I began to listen.' He glanced at the teenagers who looked down at the table. 'Two of them were explaining how they started a fire at the café two weeks ago.

'They seemed very proud of themselves and were really showing off about it. I came quickly out of the office and stood listening. When they realised that I was there, they clammed up, but I'd heard enough.'

No-one spoke, so Ian carried on. 'I told them they could write out a confession and I'd deal with it, or we could go to the headmaster and probably the police.' He reached into his pocket and brought out two sheets of paper. He handed them to Poppy who spread them out on the table.

'Why did you do such a stupid and

dangerous thing?' asked Chris, angrily.

'Just getting our own back,' one boy muttered. 'They threw us out of here.'

'We only meant to start a little fire,' said the younger boy.

'Luckily no-one was hurt,' said Poppy, 'but it was a wicked thing to do.'

'They're sorry, really,' said Mrs Goodall.

'They've been punished,' said their father. 'They're not going out with their friends for a month. And if you'll give me a bill, they'll pay for the damage out of their pocket money, however long it takes.'

'We're sorry, Miss, we didn't think,' said the older boy.

The father cleared his throat. 'We've come to ask you not to go to the police. They're not really bad boys and we don't want them to get a record.' He looked beseechingly at Poppy, who looked across at Chris.

'We won't go to the police,' he said, 'but I think they need an extra punishment. As they're not going out with their friends for the next few weeks, they can come here. Every Saturday and Sunday morning, they can come here and work hard for a few hours.'

'Don't worry about the bill,' said Poppy to Mr Goodall, as he stood up to leave, 'Mr Mabey has seen to the repairs.'

The man took her hand and shook it gratefully. 'Thank you,' he said simply, 'we've been so worried.'

As the family walked down the drive, Ian turned to Poppy and Chris. 'Thanks, both. I'll see they're here by eight-thirty on Saturday. And find some really awful jobs for them.' He grinned, waved and set off after the others.

Chris closed and locked the door. 'Was that all right?' he asked. 'You didn't think I was taking over, did you?' He looked worried.

'I can't think of a better punishment,' said Poppy. 'You did the right thing.'

★   ★   ★

The day of the wedding dawned bright and sunny. The tearoom was closed to the public because all the tables were needed for wedding guests.

The wedding breakfast was planned for twelve-thirty, but Ella arrived very early to start her preparations.

The tables were laid with crisp yellow tablecloths, on which, circles of white lace had been laid. On the back of each chair was a yellow and white flower posy.

Chris has taken home two baskets of flowers the night before and Ella had worked for several hours to create the dainty table decorations she now placed carefully in each table centre. Alongside, she placed little white china dishes filled with pale yellow bonbons.

'It looks a picture,' said Poppy, placing vases of yellow forsythia on the windowsills. 'I hope they won't mind silk flowers, but it's too late for the real ones and they do look so dramatic.'

'Even if it wasn't a sunny day, it would look sunny in here,' said Ella.

Then she turned a worried face to her friend. 'I do hope they like it.'

'I should be amazed if they don't,' Poppy answered. 'Anyway, you'll soon know. Here they come.'

There was a commotion outside the door. Amidst general laughter, they heard Mr Bevington Wood say, 'Well I hope you don't want me to carry you over this threshold.'

The door burst open and the wedding party burst in.

'Well!' Mrs Mabey, now Mrs Bevington Wood looked around the room. 'This is lovely. You have worked hard. I adore it.'

Ella beamed with pleasure and conducted the bride and groom to their table, the bride still exclaiming at the prettiness of the decorations.

'And they're dressed to match it all.' Mr Bevington Wood indicated the yellow blouses and white aprons of the staff. 'Miss Poppy, you've done us proud.'

'This is all Ella's idea.' Poppy swept her arm around. There was a burst of applause from the guests who had seated themselves and were chatting happily.

The girls went into the kitchen to collect the trays of salmon mousse with lemon sauce which they had prepared for starters.

Annoushka began to giggle. 'My grandmother would feel like a queen in such a dress,' she said, looking at Mrs Bevington Wood. 'She always wears black.'

The party was in full swing. The food had been eaten and enjoyed. Poppy and Ella, faces flushed with the numerous compliments they'd received, decided to leave the clearing up until the guests had gone, and join in the fun.

Jim and Mr Bevington Wood had made entertaining speeches and now the guests were dancing enthusiastically in the small space in the middle of the room.

Jim, to prove how fit he was, was energetically propelling Poppy round the room. As they passed the outside door, it opened and a large figure stood in the doorway.

'What a noise,' said Andrew. 'Whatever is going on?'

8

Poppy sat opposite Andrew in a corner of the White Lodge Hotel. It was an hour's drive from their homes, but Andrew didn't want to be disturbed by people who might recognise them. They had a lot to discuss.

Poppy looked round the white-panelled dining-room with its gold and white French-style furniture. Huge gold framed mirrors lined the walls and added to the light in the room. The circular tables were laid with deep green tablecloths and napkins.

'What an elegant room,' she said. 'Have you been here before?'

'No,' said Andrew. 'But I agree, it is elegant.'

'I wonder whether they have a large garden?' Poppy looked towards the window.

'Poppy. Much as I appreciate your

efforts to make polite conversation, I brought you here for a purpose.'

Poppy picked up her glass of wine and looked at him over the rim.

'I have so much to say to you, I don't know where to start,' Andrew admitted.

'Perhaps you should start with where you've been and why,' Poppy suggested. 'You caused a lot of worry.'

'To you?'

'Of course. And to Annie. And the staff at your garden centre.'

'I've spoken to Dad and Annie. I'll get round to my other apologies tomorrow. For now, I want to explain to you.'

A waiter appeared at his elbow. Andrew took the menus he carried and handed one to Poppy. 'The food here is rather good, I believe. Did you eat much at the wedding?'

'I intended to,' she admitted, 'but your sudden arrival took away my appetite.'

Since his appearance at the tearoom, she had felt her spirits lift. Even before he spoke to her, she knew everything was going to be all right.

He'd kissed his grandmother and shaken hands with Mr Bevington Wood, hugged Annie and Jim, then come straight over to where Poppy had been watching from the kitchen door.

Poppy, conscious that all eyes were upon them, had led the way into the kitchen.

'Poppy.' Andrew had taken both her hands in his. 'We can't talk now. Will you let me take you out tonight, somewhere quiet, somewhere where we can be alone?' His dark eyes looked down into hers. She felt her heart beat faster. 'We must talk,' he said, and lifted her hands to his lips.

He'd left, and the rest of the day had passed in a dream. She'd performed her share of the clearing up, scarcely aware of what was happening around her. Ella, understanding, had talked little.

At last Poppy was able to go home and prepare for the evening. Slipping beneath a blanket of warm, scented bubbles in her bath, she'd wondered what Andrew would say.

It was impossible to imagine where he had been for the past few days, but she thought she knew why he'd gone. He'd been pulled in so many directions since his father's removal to hospital that indecision had driven him to flight.

But the expression in his eyes as he looked deep into hers had shown that Selena was no part of his solution.

'And perhaps I am,' she whispered to herself.

Now, in the White Lodge Hotel, she was conscious of Andrew looking at her in a quizzical way.

'I'm sorry, did you say something?' she asked. 'I was miles away.'

'No. I was just watching the different expressions on your face. What were you thinking?'

'Oh,' she blushed, 'this and that. I was thinking of the moment you arrived in the middle of the wedding party. You certainly surprised everyone.'

'Especially you.'

'Certainly me — though I think I knew you'd be back soon.'

'Did you really?' He leaned back in his chair. 'Didn't it occur to you that I might never come back?'

'No.' She said, simply. 'All you love is here — Jim, Annie, the business. I knew you couldn't turn your back on everything.'

Andrew smiled at her. 'I suppose I'd better start at the beginning,' he sighed. 'As you know, I took Selena and her French friend,' he said the words with obvious distaste, 'out to lunch. Please believe I knew nothing about them coming that day.'

She nodded. 'I know.'

'Selena started on again about the French café,' he said, wearily. 'On and on she went, every now and then appealing to Henri to back her up. Their plans would have ruined everything you've built up.'

I knew that from the start, Poppy said to him, silently. Why didn't you realise it?

Again he read her thoughts. 'You knew what it would mean, didn't you,' he said. 'I don't know why I let her talk about it when she was here.'

Poppy poured some coffee. Andrew added cream to his and watched as the cream slowly blended with the black coffee. He seemed to be thinking deeply.

'I suddenly saw Selena for what she was,' he said, quietly, 'scheming, argumentative, aggressive, everything I dislike in a woman. How I put up with her for so long I'll never know.'

He was silent for so long that Poppy asked, 'So what happened?'

'Something snapped inside me. I stood up and said, 'Thank you for the advice. I won't take it and I hope I never see you again. Goodbye', and I walked out.'

Poppy began to laugh. She couldn't help it. She tried to stop but it bubbled up and after a minute, Andrew joined in.

'I'd love to have seen Selena's face,'

she said, when she could speak. 'I don't suppose anyone has ever spoken to her like that before.'

'I'm afraid it was very rude, but I couldn't help it.'

'What did you do then?'

'I drove to Deerham Woods. There's a very quiet car park there. I sat in the car and thought, for about two hours.'

Poppy watched him intently but said nothing.

'I knew it was time to make some decisions,' he said. 'I'd made one — to get rid of Selena — now I had to decide about the garden centre and Dad and my career in computers and . . . ' he paused and looked at her, 'other things. I needed to get away for a few days, somewhere where I could plan the rest of my life. I went home, packed a case and left.'

'Without telling anyone?'

'I didn't want to make explanations and I didn't want to be influenced. I knew everything would be all right at Bramleys with Chris in charge.'

'Where did you go?'

'Cornwall.'

'Cornwall? No-one thought of that. You haven't any connection with Cornwall, have you?'

'My friend, Tony, has a cottage on the north coast, a tiny, primitive place, remote, just what I wanted. I walked on the beach and on the cliffs. Sometimes I saw no-one all day. I thought — and I made decisions.'

'What . . . what did you decide?' She asked.

'I'm going to stay and work with Dad. He needs help after his illness. Computers and a life in the city are not for me. I belong here. I like to work with my hands, to run the soil through my fingers, to plant seeds, to watch things grow.'

Poppy's eyes filled with tears. 'Oh, Andy, I'm so pleased.' She suddenly realised she'd used his old name. He didn't seem to care.

He took her hands across the table. 'I made another decision. To see more of you, to renew our old friendship — if you'll let me.'

'Oh, Andy,' she breathed, 'it's what I want more than anything.'

He stood up and came round to her chair, taking her jacket from the back and draping it round her shoulders. 'Come along. You wanted to see the garden.'

The garden wasn't large, but was thoughtfully designed. Hedges screened wooden benches, subtly lit, where couples could be alone.

They circled the garden, enjoying the gentle evening scents of the plants, then Andrew led her to a bench overlooking a small pool. A tiny fountain played in the centre. Poppy thought she would never hear the soft splash of water again without remembering that evening.

The moon came out. The garden was silent as if it held its breath. Poppy sat, encircled by Andrew's arm, afraid to speak in case she broke the spell.

At last, Andrew said, 'Have you forgiven me, Poppy?'

'Forgiven you? You mean because you went away without telling me? Of course. You had so much to think about. And I knew you'd be back.'

'You are a sweet girl.' He kissed the top of her head. Then he put a finger under her chin, tilted her face up to his and pressed his lips to hers.

'We'd better go now. It's getting late. Mrs Beaton will wonder where you are.'

He pulled her to her feet and hand in hand, they slowly strolled towards the gate.

*   *   *

As she prepared for bed, Poppy told Mrs Beaton about her evening.

'He didn't actually say he loves me, but he does, I know he does. I could feel it.'

The cat rolled over on the coverlet and blinked yellow eyes at Poppy.

'And Selena has finally gone,' said Poppy, brushing her hair. 'Gone never to return. No more ideas of a French café. Everything will be as it was before.'

She picked up the large cat and placed her in a basket at the side of the bed.

Sometime during the night, Mrs Beaton would jump lightly up and settle herself against Poppy's back until morning.

★   ★   ★

Andrew delivered the invitations to dinner with Jim and Annie, the next day.

'Tomorrow night, about seven-thirty,' he said. 'You can come, can't you? They said they have something important to tell us both together. They were smiling and looking very mysterious.'

Poppy was pleased to accept the invitation. She had seen little of Jim since he came back from the seaside. He was busy taking up the reins again at work.

Ella looked up and smiled knowingly.

Annie, in a dress of deep gold, opened the door to Poppy and seemed to be containing her excitement with difficulty.

Jim and Andrew lounged, glasses in hand, in the drawing-room. They both greeted her with a kiss and Jim hurried to pour her a drink.

'We're ready,' said Annie. 'The twins are out for the evening, so we can eat and talk in peace.'

'Eat first,' said Jim, 'then we can concentrate on talking.' He smiled at Poppy, and tucking her hand under his arm, led her into the dining-room.

Annie enjoyed entertaining and though Poppy and Andrew were the only guests, she had gone to a lot of trouble to create a beautiful table.

Ivy sprays twined around white candles and across the gleaming white table-cloth. Glasses sparkled and cutlery shone.

Slices of scarlet tomatoes sprinkled with fresh mint, awaited them on the table.

'These are from the garden centre, aren't they?' said Poppy. 'I recognise the flavour.'

'They are indeed. Everything is home grown here,' said Jim, with pride.

The roast chicken which followed was soft and tender. Annie had cooked small new potatoes and fresh green peas to go with it. It was just the sort of meal Poppy enjoyed best.

She helped Annie to carry out the dishes, then brought in the meringue nests filled with cream and raspberries.'

'Our raspberries too,' said Andrew. 'I've been thinking, why don't we develop the fruit and vegetable section? We do it on a very small scale at present, but fresh food which hasn't travelled from the other side of the world is very popular now.

'Why don't we make a feature of it — use that wasted corner where the small garden ornaments are? We could put in counters and fixtures and . . . ' he was well away, his face shining with enthusiasm.

'Hold your horses,' said his father. 'We're going to discuss that sort of thing when we have our coffee. Now then, inside or out?'

'The wind's blowing up outside,' warned Annie. 'It might be cold. Let's go into the lounge and make ourselves comfortable.'

When they were all seated with coffee cups at hand, Jim looked at his wife. 'Shall I tell them, or you?'

'It's your decision. You start. I'm sure I shall join in.'

Jim laughed. 'Try to stop you. Well then,' he looked at Andrew. 'I enjoyed my weeks with Pauline — didn't miss this place as much as I thought I would. When Annie came down to see me, we went for long walks by the sea and we found we really liked it. So much so that . . . ' he looked at Annie.

She leaned forward excitedly. 'We've bought a house, not far from the hotel.'

'A summer place,' said Andrew. 'What a good idea.'

'No,' Jim broke in. 'Not a summer place.'

'You mean ... you mean you're going to live at Porthaven? Permanently?'

Annie smiled. 'It's a beautiful house. You'll love it. And plenty of bedrooms for visitors.' She looked across at Poppy. 'You must both come down often.'

'What about the twins?' asked Poppy. 'They're settled at school here, aren't they?'

'There's a good sixth form college at Porthaven. They can go there. And they'll be at university in a few years.'

Andrew sat back in his chair. He didn't look pleased. His father looked at him inquiringly.

'I've just sorted out my future,' said Andrew. 'I've given up my life in computers to help you here and now you're going to sell the place.' He stood up, walked over to the window and stood with his back to the room.

Poppy looked with concern from Andrew to the older couple.

'Andrew, come and sit down,' said Jim. 'Can't you see what it means. I'm handing over Bramleys to you. You can run it as you like — develop your fruit and vegetable sales — anything. I have complete faith in you. I won't interfere.'

Andrew spun round. Poppy caught a glint in his eyes which she thought might be a tear. She ran to him and threw her arms round him.

'Oh, Andrew, I'm so pleased for you. What a wonderful opportunity.'

Andrew returned her hug, then looked at his parents. 'I don't know what to say. I don't deserve it.'

Poppy went back to her chair and busied herself with her coffee cup. She felt tears in her eyes too.

'I'm glad you're both pleased,' said Jim. 'You two will have to work closely together.' He and Annie exchanged amused glances which Poppy pretended not to see.

'So you're happy to take over?' Jim asked his son. 'Good. There's no rush, but we'll have a lot of discussions in the next few weeks.'

'I have some news too,' said Poppy, shyly. 'I have enough money now to buy my tearoom — if you are still agreeable.' She looked anxiously at Jim.

'That's wonderful, Poppy,' the older man said. 'We'll go and see Arvon, my solicitor, next week.'

Poppy and Annie smiled happily at each other then Poppy glanced at her watch. 'I'm sorry to break up the evening but I must go home now and get some sleep. If I can, with so much to think about.' She caught Andrew's eye and they smiled at each other.

He jumped up. 'I'll come with you. I can do with some air.'

'But I've brought my car.'

'No problem. I'll walk back. Do me good.'

In the car, Andrew leaned his head back and closed his eyes.

'I've got so many ideas whirling around,' he said. 'I don't know where to begin.'

They drove in silence until they

reached Poppy's house. 'You can't come in,' she said. 'We'll begin to talk and never get any sleep.'

He wrapped his arms around her and held her close. 'So many ideas,' he repeated. 'Together we'll make it the best garden centre in the area.'

'Together?'

'I see your tearoom as an important focal point. More important than it is now,' he said, hastily. 'We could open the whole place until eight o'clock, several nights a week. Gardening is a growing hobby. People who work don't just want to come at weekends. We could encourage them to come in the evenings.'

Poppy was silent, thinking of the implications. Did she want to be there twelve hours a day?

Andrew sat up, moving his arms away from her. 'I'm not saying I have any time for Selena's ideas,' he said, 'but perhaps we could do something along those lines for just two or three nights a week.'

'I don't want anything to do with Selena's ideas,' said Poppy. 'And you said you didn't either.'

'I know,' he said, soothingly, 'but it might make sense to diversify a little.'

'Diversify into a French restaurant,' she said. 'No thank you.' She reached across him and opened his door. 'There's no point in this discussion. Thank you for this evening. Now if you don't mind, I want to put my car away.'

'So you won't even discuss it?'

'Goodnight, Andrew.' Poppy stared ahead through the windscreen, refusing to look at him.

After a few minutes, he got out.

'Goodnight, Poppy,' he said coldly. 'I expect I'll see you tomorrow.'

Dashing the tears from her eyes with her fingers, Poppy turned the car into the space at the side of her cottage. Would she never be free of Selena? In a few minutes, her happy evening had turned to ashes.

9

Three days later, Poppy and Jim were sitting in the office of Mr Arvon. The solicitor, tall and thin, with small spectacles on the end of his nose, showed no surprise when the situation was explained to him.

'So my boy will run the business and Poppy will own her own café. And we hope they'll work happily together.' Jim patted Poppy's hand and she gave him a shy smile.

'It's good to see young people taking on responsibilities,' said the solicitor. He looked down at the desk. 'I think I have all the information I need. I'll have the papers ready for you both to sign in a few days — say Friday morning?'

Jim and Poppy stood up.

'You're off to the seaside then,' said Mr Arvon, accompanying them to the door.

'We are indeed.' Jim's smile was wide. 'Annie is so excited. She lived near the sea as a child and she can't wait to get back.'

Outside, Jim looked at his watch. 'Can you stay away for another hour?'

Poppy nodded. 'Ella's enjoying being in charge. She won't want to see me back too soon.'

'Right then.' Jim took her arm. 'Lunch.' They crossed the road to a mock Tudor inn on the opposite corner.

'There's not a great choice of food,' said Jim, 'but it's well cooked and there's plenty of it.'

When they were settled at a table near the fireplace, which was filled with artificial flowers rather than logs, he gave Poppy a serious look.

'I'm not one to beat about the bush,' he said, 'so I'll come right out with it. Have you and Andrew quarrelled? When you left us the other evening, you both looked so happy. You were smiling and chatting together like really close friends. Now he's moping about the place and you've hardly smiled this morning.'

Poppy thought for a moment. She might as well tell Jim what had happened. He'd always been support-ive; he wouldn't blame her now.

'We did have an argument,' she admitted, 'when he took me home. Everything was fine, and then he started on again about the French restaurant.'

Jim slapped a hand on the table. 'Can't he leave well alone. That Selena again! I thought she was out of his life.'

'Oh, she is,' Poppy assured him. 'I'm sure of that. And he didn't say that he wanted to use her ideas, just that it might be a good idea to think of diversifying.'

'You're being very fair,' said Jim, 'but you don't agree with him?'

'We've been over it so many times,' said Poppy with a sigh. 'I like my café the way it is and so do my customers. Andy is ambitious. He doesn't want to stand still. He said he had so many ideas whirling around.'

'He'll have to proceed slowly.' Jim's face wore a worried frown. 'I'm giving him the business but there's not a great deal of money. I have the rest of the family to think about. He'll have to build the place up before he splashes out.'

When she got back to the tearoom, Poppy discovered that Ella and Annoushka had had a very busy morning.

'I'm sorry,' she said, feeling guilty about the lunch with Jim.

'We enjoyed it,' said her friend. 'Time flew by. Annoushka worked so hard and her English is really improving.'

Poppy smiled at the Polish girl. 'Thank you, Annoushka. Would you like to finish early today? Go now and have a few hours off.'

When the girl had left, Poppy sat down opposite Ella. 'I need to talk,' she said. 'I don't want advice exactly, just to get my thoughts straightened out.'

Ella poured two cups of tea and handed one to Poppy without comment.

'Andy won't let go of this French restaurant idea,' said Poppy. 'He has big ideas and the café is part of them.'

'But this place will soon be yours,' objected Ella. 'He can't force you to do anything.'

'Force doesn't come into it. He's hoping to persuade me.' Poppy poured milk into her cup and stirred slowly. 'Am I being selfish or short-sighted about this? Am I objecting merely because Selena had the idea first? What should I do?'

'Is that a rhetorical question?'

'No. Tell me what you think. I do need some advice.'

Ella was silent for a while, thinking. 'You should forget Selena, forget that it was originally her idea and talk to Andrew,' she said at last. 'Selena has gone now. You and Andrew must make the decisions that suit you both.'

'So I should give in?'

'That's not the right attitude. If you want the place to be a success, you must forget the past and work out the future. And the future belongs to you and Andrew.'

Poppy looked out of the window. She didn't answer, but Ella saw her face soften. Then she turned to her friend. 'The wise woman of Bramleys Garden Centre,' she said, with a gently mocking smile. 'Is it because you're married? Does that help you to see both sides?'

'Compromise is certainly important in marriage,' said Ella. 'Try discussion before you make a decision.'

When Ella had gone home, Poppy decided to make up for the time she had spent away in the morning and fill out some order forms. But before she could start, there was a knock at the kitchen door. She unbolted and opened it and discovered Andrew with his arms full of folders.

'May I come in?' he asked.

'Of course,' she stood aside for him to enter. He studied her and she felt glad she hadn't changed from the pink summer suit she'd worn to visit the solicitor.

'You look very pretty in that colour,' said Andrew, 'like a rose.'

'Thank you.' She looked up at him and his eyes, warm and glowing, looked deep into hers. Confused, she made a space on the table. 'Would you like to put your folders down?'

'I've been with Dad. He says we should talk.'

'Ella says the same thing.'

He grinned at her. 'Then perhaps we should.' He pulled out a chair for her. 'These are my plans — some of them. A few sketches and notes.'

'The ideas that were whirling around?' she suggested. 'Caught and put down on paper.'

'Exactly. Not all of them, of course. I've just made a start.'

He drew several sheets of paper from a folder and spread them across the table. Poppy picked up one and studied it. 'It looks like a series of little rooms,' she said at last. He looked pleased.

'That's just what it is. They'll be built around the edge of the garden centre on the south and west sides. Each little room will show a different range of garden ideas and products. See. This one has granite sculpture and granite flint paths. This has a small water feature and curved stone benches. This features different types of wood.'

'Like the small gardens at the Chelsea Flower Show,' said Poppy.

'These will be even smaller, of course, but along the same lines.'

She turned a shining face to him. 'This is really exciting, Andy. When will you start?'

'At once,' he said, catching her enthusiasm. 'Chris likes the idea too. He'll be working on quite a lot of it.'

'Are you going to develop your market garden idea?'

'Yes. That's another scheme scheduled for immediate development.' He pulled out another sketch and handed it to her. 'I've been to see several growers nearby and they're keen. It will be all local produce.'

Poppy replaced the papers on the table. 'It's so exciting,' she said. 'What does Jim think?'

'He's all for it. But . . . ' he looked directly at her, 'he wants us to work together — happily.'

'Andy.' Poppy looked down at her hands which were clasped together on the table as if she wanted to stop them from trembling. 'I've been thinking. Perhaps we should discuss your French café idea.'

'Poppy! Oh, Poppy.'

'But . . . ' she broke in, hastily. 'I'm not willing to alter the tearoom. This would have to be an additional venture. It would need a lot of discussion and planning to find the right way to approach it.'

She looked up to find Andy looking at her with a strange expression on his face. Slowly he stood up and pulled her to her feet.

'My darling, Poppy,' he whispered and drew her into his arms. Poppy closed her eyes and felt his lips against

159

her forehead and then her mouth, pressing gently then with increased fervour. 'I've wanted to do that for a long time,' he said, at last. 'Did you mind?'

'Mind?' She smiled. 'I've wanted it too.'

'My sweet Poppy.' Their lips met again and their arms tightened around each other.

'Come and see the centrepiece of the garden,' he said at last. 'It's at a very early stage but I can explain it to you.'

They strolled across the lawn to the garden where, beyond the office, Poppy could see that an area had been cleared and curved stone benches arranged in a circle.

'I've ordered a small pyramid to stand in the middle of the benches,' said Andrew, 'then there'll be a walk of granite chippings around it then a circle of scented roses. What do you think?'

'It sounds lovely.' Poppy stepped across the walk and sat on one of the benches. 'I can smell the roses.' She closed her eyes.

At that moment, the moon slipped from behind a cloud and shone full on the garden. Poppy opened her eyes and gazed up at it.

In a moment, Andrew was beside her on the bench. 'You look like a beautiful statue in the moonlight. It's no good, I can't deny my feelings any longer. I love you. Say you love me, too. We've had arguments, but they're in the past. I think I've always loved you, but I've only realised it now.' He gazed beseechingly at her.

Poppy twined her arms about his neck. Was he really saying the word she'd waited so many years to hear?

'Darling Andy, of course I love you,' she answered.

'Then will you marry me?'

'Of course I will.' She gazed into his eyes. 'Could you doubt it?'

'I've got everything I ever wanted,' he said a few minutes later. 'There's nothing left to wish for.'

'This is where wishes end and work begins.' Poppy snuggled closer in his arms.

Jim couldn't stop smiling on Friday when he took Poppy to the solicitor's office to sign the papers which would make her the undisputed owner of Poppy's Tearoom.

'It's what I always dreamed of,' he said, 'what Annie and I always dreamed of — you and Andy together. And he's so happy. Goes about humming to himself with a daft grin on his face.'

'We haven't got round to discussing the French restaurant yet,' she warned. 'Just because I'm going to marry him, I'm not going to give in. My tearoom remains my tearoom.'

They were sitting in a little café near to Mr Arvon's office, drinking coffee and eating buttered teacakes. Poppy poured them each another cup of coffee.

'Don't look so fierce,' said Jim. 'Have another teacake.'

Poppy grinned at him. 'You've got

butter on your chin. But I mean it. Now that I've got the papers,' she patted her handbag, 'the tearoom's all mine.'

'I've been thinking,' said Jim, 'and I've come up with a few ideas. I want to discuss them with someone first, not Andy, then I'll tell you. In the meantime, don't you two start any more arguments.'

* * *

When the lunchtime crowd had gone on the Wednesday of the following week, Mr and Mrs Bevington Wood came into the tearoom looking pleased with themselves.

'They're up to something,' Poppy whispered to Ella. 'Look at their faces.'

Tea and cakes were ordered and ten minutes later, Jim and Annie appeared and joined them.

'Family gathering.' Poppy smiled at them as she took their order.

'Just finalising a few things,' said Jim,

vaguely, taking a notebook from his pocket.

Poppy gave him a quizzical look and returned to the kitchen. 'Yes, they're definitely up to something,' she said.

Andrew's family sat in a huddle for the next hour. There was much serious talking and a few laughs, but Poppy, despite her frequent journeys past their table, was unable to make out the subject of their discussion. At last they all stood up, ready to leave.

'Can you come over this evening, Poppy?' asked Annie, casually.

'I could come about eight. Is it for anything special?'

'We think so,' said Andrew's grandmother. 'But we won't tell you now. We'll see you at eight.'

The family assembled in the drawing-room when Poppy arrived just after eight.

Jim sat at a small table, shuffling papers. When everyone was seated, he stood up. 'I shall be spokesman as it was my idea,' he began, 'but we're all,' he gestured around, 'part of it.'

Poppy looked at Andrew. 'I'm in the dark as much as you,' he said. 'Come on, Dad, what's all this about?'

'First, let me say that we're all delighted that you and Poppy have decided to marry. And when you're married, you'll run the garden centre between you, and I'm sure, make a great success of it.'

'Here, here,' growled Mr Bevington Wood.

'I know that Andrew wants the catering side of the business to be just as important as the rest,' Jim went on. 'So we four,' he smiled at the others, 'put our thinking caps on, and came up with an idea. You two may not like it,' he warned the young couple, 'but if you do, it will be our combined wedding present to you.'

'You're being very mysterious,' said Poppy.

Jim sat down and leaned back in his chair.

'What we propose,' he said, 'is to

build another restaurant backing on to your tearoom. It would probably be open three or four evenings a week. The two staffs would share the kitchen, but as you wouldn't be open at the same time, that shouldn't matter. You'd each have your own fridges and freezers and so on — we can settle those details later.'

'It would mean that the tearoom wouldn't change,' said Mrs Bevington Wood, eagerly.

'We'd still have our good English food,' said her husband.

'But Andrew could try out his French ideas in the new restaurant,' said Jim.

'Who would run the restaurant?' asked Poppy eagerly.

'You'd engage a chef and other staff,' said Jim.

'Poppy and I need to talk about it,' said Andrew, 'but it's a very generous offer. How long would it take to set up?'

'The builders who rebuilt the kitchen after the fire were most efficient,' Annie put in.

'I thought of them too,' said Jim. 'With good weather, we'd hope to have it done by Christmas.'

'There's the wedding to arrange,' said Andrew's grandmother, with a smile at Poppy. 'Will it be soon?'

Poppy blushed. 'We haven't decided.'

'And our move,' said Annie. 'But we could wait a while if necessary.'

'Looks as if we'll all have a busy year,' said Jim.

'Half year,' said Andrew. 'It's July already.' He stood up, pulling Poppy to her feet. 'We'll go now, we have some big decisions to make.'

'How long will it take?' asked Jim.

The young couple looked at each other. 'Not long,' said Andrew. 'Shall we see you here tomorrow — at eight?'

In the garden, Poppy shivered.

'Cold?' Andrew wrapped his arms around her.

'No, it's just that things seem to be moving so fast.'

They walked in silence for a few minutes, then Andrew asked, 'What do you think of their idea?'

'It's very generous.'

'But do you think it could work? Shall we agree?'

Poppy looked up into his face. 'I said I would consider the idea. I shan't go back on that. If you want it, then so do I.'

He gave her a hug. 'Right. Then we'll go for it.' They turned and strolled back to Poppy's car. 'Do you want a big wedding?' he asked. 'Bridesmaids and organ and bells and so on?'

She shook her head emphatically. 'Definitely not a big wedding. I have very little family, only my brother and a few cousins. My brother will be home on leave from the army in late September — could we have the wedding then?'

'If we can wait that long.'

'Ella will want to arrange the reception,' Poppy smiled.

'In your tearoom?'

'Of course. Where else?'

He opened the car door and she slid

into the driving seat. 'So there's nothing more to discuss' he said, with a wide smile. He bent to kiss her through the open window.

'Nothing more,' she agreed, returning his kiss. 'Our future is sealed.'

10

On a fine September morning, Poppy and Andrew were married at the small Norman church in the village.

'You look radiant, my dear,' said Mrs Bevington Wood, 'and I love your dress.'

Poppy smoothed the heavy figured cream satin of her skirt and buried her face in the cream and gold roses of her bouquet. 'You were right about white,' she said. 'Cream seems much more appropriate for early autumn.'

'You look lovely.' Mr Bevington Wood joined them. 'Brings a tear to my eye.' He dabbed his eyes, theatrically.

'Come along, darling.'

Andrew took Poppy's arm. 'Photographs.'

Chris and Poppy's brother, Robert, were rounding up the guests and after much jostling and changing of places, the photographs were taken.

Then the wedding party strolled the few hundred yards through the village and on to the garden centre.

Ella had supervised the décor in the tearoom. Huge bowls of cream and gold roses scented the air and garlands of cream satin ribbon decorated the chairs and windows.

She had recruited extra helpers who were now busily carrying trays from table to table, placing the cold first course before each guest.

Despite Poppy's protests, her friend insisted on overseeing the rest of the meal in the kitchen. Only when they reached the final course did she agree to join the wedding group again, to a round of applause from everyone and a hug from Poppy.

Andrew, handsome, proud and confident made a witty speech. Chris, as best man, stood up to reply. He was shy of speaking in public, so it was very short. But immediately, Jim jumped to his feet.

'Just a few words,' he protested, in answer to shouts from the floor for him to sit down. 'I must tell everyone how happy I feel that Andrew is marrying our lovely little Poppy. Of course,' he said complacently, 'I knew years ago that it would happen, but the young 'uns only thought of it a few months ago.' There was laughter from the guests.

'When they get back from their honeymoon, Annie and I will be going to our new house by the sea. They can move in to our house here and take over everything. And the very best of luck to them.'

He sat down amid much applause. Poppy slipped from her chair and went down the table to give him and Annie a kiss. Andrew joined her.

'We're going to slip away now,' he said. 'The tables and chairs must be moved for dancing. Can you supervise it?'

Jim clasped his son in his arms then embraced Poppy. 'Leave it to me. Off you go and have a wonderful time.

Come and see us when you get back.'

Ella appeared and Poppy gave her a hug. 'Take care of Mrs Beaton, won't you,' said Poppy. 'Tell her I'll be back in a week.'

She and Andrew crept into the kitchen, out of the back door and down to his car. But sharp eyes had spotted them from the window and the guests streamed out of the tearoom. As Andrew swung the car out of the gate, Poppy threw her bouquet behind her, where it was caught by a delighted Annoushka.

Andrew took Poppy's hand and kissed it.

'Happy, Mrs Mabey?' he asked.

'Very happy,' she answered.

'Provence, here we come,' said Andrew.

★   ★   ★

MR AND MRS ANDREW MABEY PROUDLY ANNOUNCE THE OPENING OF THEIR NEW EVENING RESTAURANT, THE CAFÉ DES FLEURS.

It was a cold, crisp December evening three weeks before Christmas. Poppy, in a lavender blue long dress which she'd bought for her honeymoon, and Andrew, in a dinner jacket and bow tie, stood in the centre of the dining-room of the Café des Fleurs

'It's quite beautiful,' said Poppy. 'I never dreamed we'd be ready in time.'

'We could be back in Provence,' said Andrew, 'the colours, the ornaments, everything is right.'

The walls had been painted a soft, chalky blue, the carpet was red ochre and the ceiling recalled the gold of sun and sunflowers. Golden bulbs in the lamps helped to spread a Mediterranean warmth.

The tables were spread with flowered cloths and in the centre of each sat a fat wax candle in a glass holder.

Andrew led Poppy over to one of the rustic benches which stood against the wall. They relaxed for a moment against the row of bright cushions, and looked around.

'Whenever we want to think of our honeymoon, we can sit here and imagine we are back in France,' he said. 'Remember the market where we bought those wall plates?'

'And the little shop in Aix where we bought those bowls,' she said. 'And the scent of the lavender fields stretching as far as the eye could see.'

Poppy had arranged baskets of lavender in the corners of the room, and their scent vied with the delicious aroma of roast lamb with thyme and rosemary.

A man looking very like Chris came out of the kitchen. He pressed a switch and French café music flooded the room.

'Is everything ready, Rick?' asked Andrew.

Rick smiled and gave a thumbs up sign. He was Chris's younger brother, with Chris's smile but a more self confident manner. He had been working in a French vineyard for the past five years and had providentially returned a month ago. Andrew had persuaded him to stay for a few months and supervise the setting up of the Café des Fleurs.

Rick had found them a chef, Dan, who specialised in French cuisine, and the two men worked happily to organise the new venture.

Three young men dressed in black with ankle-length white aprons came out of the kitchen. Poppy laughed delightedly.

'Don't they look good! Like real French waiters. The one on the left looks familiar.'

'It's Michael Goodall.'

'Michael Goodall? Wait a minute, wasn't he the boy who . . . ?'

'Set fire to your kitchen? Yes.'

'So what is he doing here?'

'I'm giving him a chance,' said Andrew. 'His mother assures me he's turned over a new leaf.'

Poppy looked at him in amazement, then she reached up and kissed him. 'That's very kind of you. Let's hope he appreciates it.'

'Listen,' Andrew looked towards the door. He glanced at his watch.

'Yes, our guests are arriving. Are you ready, Mrs Mabey?' He led her towards the door.

Poppy felt a thrill of anticipation surge through her body. For so long, she had opposed Andrew's idea for a French café. Now she knew it was going to be a wonderful new experience for them to share.

'I'm ready,' she said.

Andrew bent and gave her a warm kiss then he flung open the door to greet the first guests of the Café des Fleurs.

THE END

We do hope that you have enjoyed reading this large print book.

Did you know that all of our titles are available for purchase?

We publish a wide range of high quality large print books including:
Romances, Mysteries, Classics
General Fiction
Non Fiction and Westerns

Special interest titles available in large print are:
The Little Oxford Dictionary
Music Book, Song Book
Hymn Book, Service Book

Also available from us courtesy of Oxford University Press:
Young Readers' Dictionary
(large print edition)
Young Readers' Thesaurus
(large print edition)

For further information or a free brochure, please contact us at:
Ulverscroft Large Print Books Ltd.,
The Green, Bradgate Road, Anstey,
Leicester, LE7 7FU, England.
Tel: (00 44) **0116 236 4325**
Fax: (00 44) **0116 234 0205**